RISE FROM A DARK FALL

RISE FROM A DARK FALL
#10

DHEERIKA PANDEY

PARTRIDGE
A Penguin Random House Company

Print information available on the last page.

To order additional copies of this book, contact
Partridge India
000 800 10062 62
orders.india@partridgepublishing.com

www.partridgepublishing.com/india

CONTENTS

To all the people who fight life with hope, love, positive attitude and a bright smile.

ABOUT THE AUTHOR

Dheerika Pandey is an author and a poet based in Delhi, India. She writes fiction and has written twenty-eight poems in Hindi as well as in English. She is presently a student of class eleven. Writing is her passion. She loves art, music, nature, animals, reading, photography, travelling, and learning new things.

Through The Tunnels Of Struggle

1#Introduction

My life has been a perfect example of struggle. In my teens, people said that women are treated same as the men. But since my childhood my own family has blamed my mother for giving birth to a girl. My elder brother was treated as a king whereas I didn't even got the place of a princess. My younger brother was also a prince. Harsh and Naksh were the two people in my house who had all the freedom. I went to school, but I knew my studies had no future. My father had a shop of grocery and Harsh would go to help him on weekends. My mother was the only one who was proud on being a mother of a girl. She was the only person who believed that no matter what Harsh and Naksh do in future, I would live happier than them. Shruti is my name! I lived in outskirts of New Delhi but to me it looked like I was living in a village.

2# School Life

I could not afford a high fee, private school. I wanted to study and had no other option than a government school. Though, all the children in my class were equally poor as me, they acted as if they were the owner of this school and I was just like a waiter to them. I had no friend except my best friend Shazia. I was neither the topper nor the failure of my class. In the eyes of my teachers I was considered one of the best students. Shazia and I were totally different, our religions were different but our thoughts matched a lot. We both knew that our families would not allow us to take up a job and work. Still we gave our best try to make our results good. Our teachers supported us a lot. They did their best efforts to clear our doubts.

3# NEIGHBORHOOD

I was blessed with good people all around me. My neighbors have always helped me and my family. Whenever my father used to taunt my mother for giving birth to a girl, Kumar uncle stopped him and asked my mother to get some water. Kumar uncle's son Aryan bhai used to tell my parents that he and his parents always wanted a girl, a daughter and a sister.

"You should be proud being a father of such a girl." Shanti aunty used to tell my parents.

Their family always helped us. When Aryan bhai got his job he took us for a ride in his new car. I wanted to be a teacher as I thought that it's the best profession. No one gets more love than a teacher. She spreads education to all. My family did not support me for this but Shanti aunty and Kumar uncle was there for me. Sharma family and Aarti didi were also like a family to us, they helped us whenever we needed transport to visit our village.

4# SHAKING EARTH

All was going well. My father had now purchased the land on which our shop was, Harsh came first in computer science and won huge amount as an award, our bank account had money as a saving. It's a saying when all is good, bad is near. This really happened. There was an earthquake that occurred at a very high scale. I was in the school as my extra classes were going on, when the earthquake came. We were told to sit under the tables. Then we heard a sound and the cottage of our security guard broke into pieces. The guard was declared dead immediately. The junior building was empty as children were safe at home. Naksh and Harsh were also at home as they were having holidays. When the earthquake stopped we found that we all were safe. Filled with joy I walked home and saw, that shops were without salesmen, the whole way was empty. For two minutes I thought I had entered the wrong area. But as I moved forward I saw bricks and cement all over the ground, the pond which used to be filled with fishes and fresh water was now filled with red blood and all houses were invisible. My house didn't existed any more. When I left in the morning Harsh and Naksh were playing (ludo) inside our room and ama (my mother) was cooking food. Now, their bodies were lying under the heavy cement. I had no idea where my father was. I went to his shop, but there was no one to attend me.

I came back and checked whether our phone was working or not. It was not.

"Shruti! Thank god your are safe."

The voice came from my back.

It was Aryan Bhai, he was safe too. He was in the same tears as me. I could understand from his face that he also lost his world like me. His next dialogue was that his father is safe and called him to inform that my father went to the South Bazaar and is no more. I could not believe it that god will give him such a big punishment. Earth had stopped moving for me. Aryan bhai could not even find his mothers dead body. It was all no less than an ugly dream.

I was saying to god "Please, stop the dream and get me back to reality."

"It's not a dream wake up Shruti" Aryan bhai said.

5# STRUGGLE TO BEAT THE REST

I had nothing left for me. I hated my father but my hatred was not to kill him, after all he gave me birth. I shouted on Naksh, I had fights with Harsh but I didn't wanted to gift them death. Sometimes I became upset with the illiteracy of my mother but it didn't meant that I wanted to see her lying dead. Why this happened to me? Now I wished that I had not gone under my desk and should have been inside the security guard's cottage and then I may also live with my family in heaven. Sharma uncle and his family was safe as they went for a trip. I contacted Aarti didi for help, she was in her office. She picked my call, listened to my story.

In the end she just said "It's a wrong no."

I could not understand why she did this to me. I took off my school bag and ran towards Shazia's house. She lived a little far from my home and also the school. After walking so much I was finally at her door. I rang the bell twice as I was in a hurry. Shazia's brother Hamad bhai opened the door. I explained him the situation. Hamad bhai took me and Shazia on his bike and helped me with the dead bodies. He could not do anything more than this for me. Aryan bhai performed all the rituals for my family and his mother. I knew Shazia won't refuse to help me. And then I realized that for how long will I stay at their house. Aryan bhai and Kumar uncle had offered me a stay in their house. I immediately wanted to say yes, but the inside in me said that the world around does not see Aryan as your brother and staying in a house with two men will give the world a chance to stare me. So I had to say a no. I could not say it so directly, as I thought they will feel a little awkward and insulted.

I answered saying "Thank you so much uncle and bhai, I am grateful to you. Actually the point is that I wanted to stay in my house no matter it's no more."

"How will you stay here?" Aryan bhai asked.

"Beta it's your choice." Uncle said.

Then we exchanged byes. I had never imagined living in my own area with no one alive around, not even the houses.

"Are you stupid or a big fool. How could you decline such a great offer? Did you lose your mind for few minutes. How will you survive in this place, without any roofs. May be you'll just spend the whole night communicating with the stars and capturing shots of night sky in your minds? You don't even have water to drink and food to be fed." My mind shouted to my soul.

The whole night I could not sleep as I had no place to lay and I sat on a piece of cement with iron rods peeping outside it. I could not believe that the people whom my father gave money and supported in their bad times were not ready to help me. Sharma uncle took loan from my father and his wife stole my Ama's gold earnings. My parents didn't wanted to make them feel guilty so they never asked these things back. But today when I asked him for help he refused by saying that he and his family will not come back to Delhi for just to help me.

6# LIGHT IN THE NIGHT

For how many days more I will stay hungry and I'll not sleep. So I decided the same night to take revenge from the world who insulted my parent's good deeds. I packed the left over safe stuff within a cloth. I went to the shop and took all the food available there. It was 3'o clock in the morning so no one noticed me doing this. I was not aware of the routes of Delhi. I kept walking thinking that I'll at least reach a place with people and buildings around. I reached the Old Delhi railway station after walking for more than hours and keeping my throat thirsty, stomach empty and head and legs in pain. I wish I had taken part in my school's race. If I can walk for more than a hour, I would have walked (ran) 300 meters race and won the award. I slept for two hours at the station. Then decided to work and collect money for my higher studies. After thinking for a while I agreed on doing multiple jobs.

7# SEARCH FOR A HOPE

To get a job and work was the only hope for me. After searching a lot of jobs I finally started working. Jobs were not the qualified ones but the under qualified ones. In the morning I cleaned around twenty cars in a society at some distance from the station, in the afternoon I worked for the same people as a maid and a cook and in the evening I helped people in the railway station with all sought of help I could do. Tourists from abroad gave me special tip as I helped them with the language problem. My earning was not the earning which could be saved for future. I used to sleep at the railway station. My guilt made me realize every night that I was doing wrong as its not permitted to sleep there. But I pushed my guilt aside as god was making me do this. I had a very little amount left with me as a saving so I decided to work more. I managed and took the responsibility of handling children of working parents in the same society. Many times I was scolded for being so much selfish for money and doing so many jobs. But no one asked the reason behind my selfishness of money. On the weekends when the working parents did not needed a baby sitter I worked in a parlor, that's also in the same society. After doing all these jobs for around there years I managed to save a good amount for my education. I was doing this because my heart and mind both knew that I was not so coward to attempt a suicide and the only way to prove I was brave was to overcome all the misery with my success which was only possible with being educated.

8# LEARNING AGAIN

I was in class tenth and 15 years was my age when my world got finished. There also came a time when I was not in any of the classes and 18 years was my age. I could not go to school to attend eleventh class and twelfth class. My dream of being a teacher had also been ruined by time. I went to a cyber cafe and searched the web. After that I decided to do a course of event management in a government college. But I had not completed my schooling which became an important fact preventing me for higher studies. My mind had a thought that will I have to do multi jobs to earn a living? Between the thoughts my phone rang. I picked it up. I had no clue who would be the caller. It was Aryan bhai ! He asked me about my life and told me he was gifted a son on the same date on which I was born, 20th January. In three years I never celebrated my birthday, his son gave me a reason to do it next time. I explained my history to him with extreme expressions. As in three years there was no one for my tears. I was glad he remembered me and my birth date. After sharing my thought on event management, he told me that his sister in law is doing the same course in a private institute. He ensured me that the costs were not too high. As I hanged his phone down, the next call was from his sister in-law Kim. She helped me to get admission in the college. A thank will never be enough for her favor on me.

9# SUCCESS

I am included in India's top 10 event managers. My company broke five records which is considered a huge thing. All this took seven years. I may be twenty-five but still in my heart hides a fifteen years old Shurti who at some point of life had lost her world. I have arranged events before for celebrities and businessmen but I got an order for the Indian cricket team for the first time. Aryan bhai told me that if this event goes the right way, it will mark my name to the top. Event went good even, the audience called me to the stage. Event which was being telecasted also included me. After the event Anuj kapoor, one of the fastest bowlers in the Indian cricket team thanked me for the great event. I didn't needed it as I was paid for this and this is my work.

Then my mind said "Leave it. It's nice if someone thanks you."

And then I answered his thanks. I didn't want to miss such an opportunity to take a selfie and his autograph too but my pride said it will show him that you are crazy and desperate. Still I asked a photo and his autograph. He smiled and clicked! He gave his autograph on a tissue as we couldn't find a paper. I was so happy. I may be the owner of two bungalows or the 'flower's' (my event management company) but I never got a chance to meet a cricket star.

Next day after the event I was going back from Mumbai to Delhi.

At the Airport a guy called my name "Shurti !" in a humble voice.

I had no guesses. For a second my heart said he may be Aryan bhai but my mind said he is in Delhi waiting for me at Delhi airport. With a question on my face I turned around. He was Anuj. Anuj the star! The question turned into a shock.

He said "Hey".

I replied "Hi" and there was silence for one minute.

Announcement for his flight and mine too was heard perfectly in that silence. The flight took off and landed safely. At luggage area I was surprised to know the we were in the same flight. He helped me talking off my luggage. I was feeling embarrassed becuase such a big star was taking out my luggage. So I immediately turned back by saying Thank you. After two days bell at my house's main door rang. On the door were the people whom I had never met. There was a beautiful lady and a handsome man who were the age of my parents (if they were alive). They asked me the permission to enter the house. I had no idea who they were. Their faces seemed that I had seen them somewhere. Just when I made them sit the bell rang again. Servant opened the door and it was Anuj again. My eyes could not believe what they saw. He called the old couple the old couple as his parents.

He introduced me to them when I served them snacks the lady said "We are not here to have food but we are here to have you."

I could not understand what she was indicating. I told her that her talks were flying above my head.

Anuj interrupted and said "Just come to the point mom."

His mother asked him to control himself. His father and mother wanted to make me their daughter. They told me that they had also bought the shagun. I was speechless.

After my silence I said "It would be my pleasure but I know my past will stop you from going further my history would make you give a second thought on me."

Anuj immediately said "We all know your past. Last night I had a talk with Aryan. We accept you as you are. Your past doesn't mean anything to us."

Words in my mind were not able to come out they were.

"But……………I ……….."

10# HAPPY ENDING

Today I am sitting on the stands of Feroshah Kotla (a stadium in new Delhi), Cheering for Anuj (My husband) along with Gaurav and Gauri (My Children). I am proud of myself and my husband. My company 'flower's' is still included in top 10. My success was concluded when my revenge was completed. Aarti didi lost her job. Sharma uncle worked in a company of California at low post which shifted it's office back to California. He was working in another company after that but as the news spread of my marriage and my fame I received calls from him and his family for help. I was on the top of the world as god had punished them. Gaurav always complaints that I favor Gauri in all their fights and the fact is that I really do as I want my daughter to be treated as a princess. This is not the end of my life but the beginning.

Finding A Better Life

1# Introduction

"Read all sought of dreams but believe in those which are possible" the best quote I have ever heard. I am Sunaina. From interesting adventures to sad tragedies, I've experienced it all. I was ten when I started learning the nature of society and till now I am not able to complete my learning. I don't remember much about my childhood. But I just remember that all the moments were much were sweet than my present. No one will believe that I made my first best friends at the age of 15. My dad was alive but he was never present. It's a saying that a daughter would like to have a husband like her father, but I don't want it ever in my dreams. I could open a shop for my awards. I have achieved around thirty awards in singing and dancing. Some people thought both of these activities had no value and I had to leave my talent aside. My brother, mother, sister and grandfather were the other members of my family.

2# Noodle-The Best Pet

When I grew up I came to know secrets, which I had never expected. As a child I was very bold but now emotions have grasped me into their web. I was promised a pet as a gift at the age of 14 and on my sixteenth birthday I finally received that gift, the moment was surprising and unbelievable. He was a poodle, therefore I named him Noodle (maybe I thought Noodle first because it rhymed). For me It was a first sight love. However, it does not matter that Susann Aunt (my neighbor) was unhappy, as she could no more come to my house asking for sugar or salt.

Next year was the one for which everyone across the globe was waiting as it was predicted that this year will have a meteor shower and thousands in fact millions of gold coins would rain to the ground. Yes, you heard it right rain of coins. Some stupid group of astrologers predicted it. And as today on the new year eve I got Noodle (its also my birthday) it had to be a double celebration. Finally I had someone to listen to me even if it was not worth listening and who would wipe off my tears.

3# Stupid Prediction

It was time for me to choose my profession and opt my stream (subject stream). Teachers told me I should take humanities (arts), Friends told me commerce and according to my parents science is the only option I have. Between this I could not decide what should I take and decided to go for science and engineering. Now, in engineering we have more sub options. So it was decided. I that I would like to become an architect. I got science and very whole hearted I accepted it. Only Noodle could understand my feelings. Time kept moving and the day came on which I had to appear for my exams. My exams (according to me) went good but the result was not up to my expectations. Also, that day came when meteor shower should had happened. People were so excited about this that most of them took a holiday from their work thinking it would be easy to catch coins. Nothing happened and the astrologers were missing. Next day, was rainy day still people thought that drops of coins would fall. But rain drops had nothing rich.

4# TAMANA—NEW TORCH LIGHT

Days kept on moving. That beautiful talent I had somehow evaporated (singing and dancing). I was studying in a good college doing my first year of engineering. And I understood the truth in my mother's saying "only 1% of school friends are remembered by us as the rest leave us, so just focus on your studies." As any other child I didn't believe her but today standing alone with this new crowd makes me realize for whom did I used to sacrifice my things, who used to praise me for all my efforts, who supported my talent and with whom I used to be with. My voice had no answer in return. But who knew that I will have a superb friend entering my life. Yup! Tamana. She looks weird, she is stupid and very cheerful. I first met her when I was in the physical education class. We saw each other first time but she waved her hand to me as if I was her friend from childhood. She came to me introduced herself and from starting till the end she didn't took a pause in her talk. Impressed with this we joined hands. Our friendship or you could say 'sisterhood' was famous in the whole college. I, in fact we did not know what was there between us which made us so close. She was a really very sensitive person Tamana told me she was hurt by many people but instead a weakness, being sensitive became her strength. In our college time she wrote quotes whenever she felt hurt or lonely. Living with her made my life adapt the same trick, difference was I wrote songs and she wrote quotes. With the share of our souls we didn't came to know when our studies were over. On the last day we promised ourselves that 'Till we die, we will not forget the one who has our heart (each other).

5# Dark Nights

Over the years where my songs were only with me, Tamana was a famous writer and had huge audience from all over the world. Good news was that we were still best friends. I am an architect and I have developed a 5.D system in architecture series. There is a saying 'when we fall from a big height we get more hurts.' Tamana had experienced it in reality. When she was coming back home from an international conference held in Mumbai, her car driver stopped the car and it was hijacked by five people. They were similar to the ones who in history had hurt her. However, they could not take the respect and position Tamana had. Within few minutes my world got shaken in an earthquake. Earthquake was the death of Tamana by five murderers. Newspaper was drained with coffee when I read the last line. I could not even meet my friend last time. I was informed very late (only through newspaper).

6# FAMILY MYSTERY

This was not enough. Evil did not leave my hand. In my room there was a note saying Don't believe the world, even your family. To understand this was tough. Next day, was another note telling me that I live a reel life not a real one. The whole week, there were notes which had something different to say each day. After seven days of stress I shared this with my mother. Her eyes were saying a lot more than her words.

She was in a shock and just shouted, "We are your parents don't think about that non -sense and useless note."

Just like you I was also feeling weird. Finally the note was not there for many days. My cute Noodle started barking aloud when we all gathered downstairs in the ground. We saw a shadow running, because of darkness shadow was not classified into a female or a male. The shadow left a gift which was an empty photo album with a note (yes again).

"We love you, come back to your family."

My mother asked Rama kaka (servant) to throw the gift. To know truth I kept on asking my mother, my family but my question made no sense to them. They could not understand how I was feeling being told that I do not have real family. That same night when I was trying my best to sleep a harsh stone entered my room through the window.

"Believe me I am your well wisher. Its for your good don't trust your family."

This was enough for me to get puzzled.

In anger I shouted on my parents "What is the truth and what is not, everything around me was a lie? For whom are you doing a favor."

I could not complete my sentence because my father shouted more louder than me. All my questions were answered in one sentence.

"We are not your parents, just get out of here."

From my ears to my legs every thing was shivering. The situation made me mad. The people whom I love for around twenty four years are not mine. Seriously! After thousands of inquiry god gave me the truth. Present parents had adopted me by sending my parents (real) to a cage. The reason was still unknown. The next day I shifted to the house provided by my office. Noodle and I had new hopes with new home.

7# My Only Supporter

Getting hurt by an outsider does not matter much. But when your own people hurt you, it feels no less than a hell. I never thought that god will take such a big revenge from me for all my mistakes. The feeling why was I the only one among millions of people? Tears kept flowing from my eyes thinking about all the nonsense which happened with me. Noodle wiped my tears with a cloth (dusting cloth) in his mouth. Dogs are not like us, they never hurt us, they are hurt by a human still they understand each and every thing we say, even if they don't understand our language.

Two days after the scene. I got an injury as another gift, my right leg was fractured. Noodle knew that I am injured, therefore handled all the work himself. I had to take off from my office. Noodle bought the newspaper to me, switched on television, opened the door, swiped the curtains and opened the window. The only thing he could not do was to make a delicious coffee, also to cook food. That eight days Noodle and Kantaben (my cook) were my only support.

8# WHAT TO STEEL?

The parents who bought me up, who grew me up did not even once contacted me. And the parents who used to send me notes, now had no concern. On 28th November, 2010 I had a robbery in my house. I was in the office. All except money, clothes, stationary and furniture was stolen. Which means only foodstuff. As from one side they were facing Noodle and his anger where the other side my racks, my money locker had two locks or maybe furniture was too heavy for them. When I returned home Noodle was sitting in his dog house and after calling him for half an hour still there was no clue of him. He thought, he could not save the stolen stuff and catch the thieves. This was the first time when Noodle did not obeyed to my order. I could not stop thinking, now what is left with me to get stolen. Nothing I didn't had a family, no joy, no well wisher, no happiness and no friends. 'Am I that poor?' my mind repeated. The huge amount of money which I am earning becomes of no use as I have nothing to invest on.

9# New Chapter

Living alone made me die every second. I married my neighbor John. He was a businessman, without a family just a cat Flow. Flow meant everything to him just like how Noodle meant the world to me. Flow and noodle had fights within few seconds. They argued on every single point and argument stayed the whole night. I invited my parents but no reply came from my family. After few months my father's closest friend came to visit me.

He looked upset and just said "I am sorry! I should had told you this earlier. Your father who gave you birth was our friend. Once he stole your father's money. It was not a small amount. And he had to send your father to the prison. He is a nice man he did not wanted you to be called an orphan so he adopted you. Your real father was sending you notes. When you shared it with your mother she became afraid to lose you. She called your real father and gave him a good amount of money to leave the city. I am sorry."

Situations were turning bad one by one. John and I decided to settle in Dubai, away from all the problems.

10# HAPPY ENDING

Dubai was a beautiful place. Amazing beaches, deserts, cuisine, buildings and that shopping festival made me spend Rs 5000 in one minute only on dresses. On 1st January, Naina and Sara entered my life. They were colors in my black and white life. We are the happiest family on earth. I have no idea where my real father is. I apologized my family on my behalf. Everything is well now, my parents visit me and our happy. My small family means the largest happiness to me.

TWIST AND TURNS

1# INTRODUCTION

Natasha commonly known as Nuts, a very beautiful girl living in a joint family, brought up in Bhopal. The story begins on 1st January 2010.

"Happy New Year!", shouts her younger brother Guru replied.

"Good Morning" her elder sister Usha replied.

After breakfast, they packed their bags and went to the school. Natasha was full of madness. She was a very interesting person. Everyone knew her because of her happiness and the craze for friends. She was very bold, she never cried and spread love with her smile all around. Nuts was a perfect A1 in academics and therefore favorite of all teachers. Everyday used to be the same till she learnt a lesson, she was asked to behave normally like a grown up girl. By following this she started behaving of a high status. It took her one year to behave properly and during this she saw a big fall in her academics.

2# Fake Or Real

Maya was Natasha's so called best friend. She was full of attitude.

After small fights Maya said "Now its enough don't talk to me, everything is finished."

And Natasha being a sincere friend said "Sorry, I will not do it again."

But Nuts never valued the real gold and was busy treasuring the stones. Purnima, a very intelligent girl who always wanted to be her best friend as she thought that Nuts's joy will make her life bright. Asha not exactly but yes she had absence of mind, she never argued with anyone and was a friend indeed for all also was Natasha's inspiration. Sobita, lovingly called 'satty' was just like a teacher for Natasha. Her one of the closest friend, Komal insulted her in front of the whole class. Natasha then fought with depression, she felt lonely and cried the whole day. From that day Nuts became a very sensitive person and she never trusted anyone. She could never understand whether the face behind a friend is fake or real.

3# Time Of Sorrow

2013 was a year full of tears and sorrow for the whole family. Natasha had lost her grand father, who left silence in the house for all. Guru did not show any respect for Nuts as he thought that like Usha, Nuts did not party the whole night, listened music, go out with friends and could not understand his generation. He never realized the age gap between his sister and him. Maya showed her the doors to get out from their friendship and finally she agreed to separate from her. Natasha's parents fought the whole night and ended up with a decision to get separated from each other. It was decided that Usha, Nuts and Guru will stay in Bhopal with a caretaker and a baby sister, their mother will live in Delhi and their father and grandmother will live in New York, United States of America.

4# HEAVEN TO HELL

When Natasha opened her eyes in the morning she saw that she was in palace, her parents were together having breakfast, Usha was reading a book and Guru was having milk. When she entered her classroom everyone clapped and welcomed her. On each desk there was a note saying 'Happy Birth Day Nuts'. Seeing this Natasha could not control her joy, the smile on her face was not willing to go back. It was just like a dream come true. Everything was going according to her wishes, Maya prepared a chocolate cake for her, where Komal had a huge birthday card in her hand. Natasha could not believe that today was her birthday. No one in the family wished her, she could not remember her birthday date.

Next morning again her parents were together preparing breakfast, Usha was reading and Guru was having milk. But when she entered her classroom everybody started laughing and then she came to know yesterday was 1st april and she was being fooled. Natasha sat on her bench and started crying. When she went back home, her mother asked her the reason behind her tears but Nuts did not reply. When she woke up in the morning, she realized it was all a dream.

5# SUMMER FUN

It was Sunday, a holiday and the beginning of summer vacations. After an adventurous dream, she received a phone call from her father asking that will the children like to visit New York. Same day, in the evening their mother called and told them that she will be coming next week, to pick them for Delhi. Natasha had understood that her mother did not wanted to be outshined by her father. And then at the door was a courier from New York with tickets and passports inside it. All children were excited and they started their packing.

Finally the day arrived and they were flying above the clouds. Holding a box of chocolates in one and flowers in the other hand stood Nuts father and grandmother to give a warm welcome to the children. All three children were thrilled with anxiety seeing them. For one whole month Natasha forgot the word sorrow. The whole family (except mother) did lots and lots of fun, they travelled to Washington and New Jersey, also visited lots of tourist spots. This was a memorable trip for everyone. Natasha, Guru and Usha were back after one month fun.

6# NATASHA IS BACK

Natasha after being hurt had stopped talking to many children, she completed all her work and worked hard. Her life only had studies, her secret best friend (her diary) and herself. She was back on the right track. Good grades, good marks, trophies and medals were in her hand again, teachers praised her and gave her the title of best student. She was prepared to make her future bright. Being back does not meant that she again became mad about friends, but it means that she was now responsible, mature and independent. Her life totally had a new start and a new story ahead. After being so sensitive she was extremely bold. Natasha knew that people in this world did not care for her feelings and emotions so she did the same. Nuts had all to be happy but what she really needed was love, support and care from everyone, especially from her family.

7# LIFE OUTSIDE

Natasha completed her graduation she took part in a national level dance competition and she was declared as the 1st runner up. Nuts wanted to do fashion designing, so she went to France for further studies in fashion, as she thought that fashion was manufactured in Paris. Her life was very simple. Natasha felt lonely so she decided to buy a pet. A German Shepherd, who she named 'Tiger'. Tiger was a part of dog classes for one year where he was trained. When Nuts went out for studies he stayed at home and handled everything in the correct way. After coming back she used to talked to tiger, share her experience of whole day, despite knowing that he didn't understands a single word. Tiger was the only one who she trusted with closed eyes. She made many friends in Paris. Every Sunday Nuts and tiger went out for a walk. After a three year course of fashion designing, she did a one year training of singing and dancing, the interesting fact was that Tiger also did the same course (till the dog's part). Doing all these courses was not enough for Natasha, so she also opted for a one year training in boxing and skating, but this time tiger went to dog school. The fee for her education was paid by the money given to her by her father as a bank balance. After doing different types of courses, she was now satisfied with her talent..

8# INDIAN ADVENTURE

Natasha came back to India after 5 years and she came to know that her elder sister Usha is married and is in California with her mother, her brother Guru is in Bangalore. The caretaker who used to be with them died in an accident two years ago. And after searching a lot she came to know that her father is no more, he died due to cancer. Nuts felt very upset after knowing all this but the other way round it did not matter a lot as before also she was alone and still she is alone. Natasha was happy with Tiger. She started her clothing business, went for international fashion shows through which she got a chance to design clothes for Bollywood celebrities. After one year she was offered a movie. It was a time full of joy for Nuts as she signed the contract and her film got hit in the box office, won twenty four awards in eleven award functions. This marked her beginning in Bollywood. Then Natasha received calls and messages from her school friends. Being a celebrity she lived a luxurious life without any attitude. And then one day when Nuts came back from her fashion show, she found that Tiger was in a deep sleep. When consulted by a doctor, it was surprising to know that he was suffering from a severe disease. Natasha spent one millions on his treatment as she could not take the risk of losing Tiger. But a big amount did not ensured Tiger's life. For once he was safe. Doctors said that if this disease attacks his body again, his body cannot fight it.

9# LOOSING A FRIEND

Seeing that her parents were unhappy getting married, Nuts decided not to get married. She very well knew that Tiger did not had a long life span and then she would be all alone again but her decision was final. To support it Natasha then adopted two girls Kaira and Samaira. It was first time for Natasha as mother so many things unpredictably went wrong.

When sixth birthday of Kaira was being celebrated Tiger lost his life. Once again the time repeated itself. Natasha's soul broke into pieces, the river flowing from her eyes could not stop. She controlled herself as she thought she had lots of responsibilities upon her. Even after Tiger's death her love for animals was the same and she bought two parrots as her new pets.

10# Happy Ending

On 15th October, Nuts was given a wonderful surprise by her kids on her thirty seventh birthday. Kaira was thirteen and Samaira was fifteen. Natasha was a well known fashion designer, famous for her work in the world. She was the happiest person on earth. Sometimes she missed her family and Tiger, but smiled seeing her children growing up. According to Nuts 'if there is good education, there is hope for everything.' She stopped writing diary because she was busy with her work and family. Last of her dairy read 'Even if I am dead, the story of my life will live forever in posterity.'

True Love For A Ball

1# Introduction

I'll not write useless things to make you feel sleepy. This is a story to be inspired. It's about my class mate Shivani.

She used to say a quote "Change the present if you aren't happy with it. If you don't, you don't have the right to regret it later."

The saying is true and it should be followed. If she didn't followed this saying she had been serving as a government officer. But she is a footballer, like everyone I was also shocked. Her struggle has paid her, her confidence has shaped her and the bad times she passed through has built her. Despite her gender and the mindset of people, she managed to become a footballer. You may not find this story an interesting one, but believe me, this story is worth reading.

2# Studious Star

Shivani didn't had much stars in her academic pocket. She was not at all studious. She was often punished by teachers for her performance in examinations. Once, she was asked by her parents that she should either study hard or the doors are always open for her to leave. The next day she was sharing this with her best friend and also trying to hide her tears. Children used to give her a weird look on the result day, but her confidence didn't permit their eyes for more than two seconds. Every other teacher used to scold her for her non-stop chat box, she had thousands of stories to share with her friends every day. Shivani tried hard to give it all on her studies but she couldn't succeed. She may not be good in studies and owe full five stars but she ruled the sports sector.

3# INSEPARABLE LOVE

I don't know it exactly, but according to her friends she had a first sight love. Football was her first sight love. As a child she was tempted for football. Girls usually like to play dolls, do drawing and coloring, sing songs, shopping and dancing. Shivani didn't liked any of these. If she had an option to play football the whole day, she would have definitely taken up that option. Also she would skip her meals to play football. She used to memorize things by relating it with football. In science when we all were trying to learn rainbow formation (spectrum), she learned it, by relating it to rainbow kick in football. She played football from the age of three. As years passed, her love and passion became more high. Shivani was a great player. Even I and other school boys did not wanted to play with her as we had the fear of losing and then going through the insult done to us. Our school reached the top position in the National Football Championship. She and her love for football are still inseparable.

4# Thick And High- Wall

The world doesn't move on our orders. Whenever we see the sky, we know we cannot achieve it but still we set the maximum limit as the sky. Shivani was confident on her passion, she knew one day she would reach the sky. And as you know nothing is easy to achieve. She had several walls in between. Firstly her own family didn't support her. Her father was happy to see a rack full of medals, but didn't encouraged her. She was compared with the other girls of family and then discouraged by taunts. Her heart knew that without family support she could not walk the stairs to success. Approximately, everyday there used to be a debate on her in her house and the decision taken was always in her mother's favor which is her opposition. Secondly, the mindset of people, we cannot change someone or someone's mindset rather we have to change ourselves. The society did not wanted to accept her as a footballer, which was a problem. Thirdly her own classmates. We all would give her bad looks. When she asked the boys to play with her, we looked at her as if she was a beggar. Her best friend had warned her, when Shivani was attracted towards football. Still Shivani crossed all these bricks successfully.

5# Learning Passion

After long fights with parents, Shivani decided to go for football coaching. Her parents were not willing to pay the fees. Somehow, she managed to do save some money and pay the fees. There were only two girls out of ten boys in her coaching. During her school days, I saw her being punished for coming late to school. Where as she was always on time for her coaching classes. Shivani ignored the idiotic thoughts of people, she thought that all of them will be answered the day she is a footballer. While she was involved in coaching and totally distracted from her studies. For almost five hours she practiced under the sun with her coach. From a fair looking girl with average weight she had transformed into a dark skin toned one with a slim body. She was as thin as a nail. It looked as if she was working on her body for years to achieve the slim look. Her studies were going down and down. Her family, teachers and relatives were thinking about it, but Shivani didn't gave a damn to what will happen if she fails in her class.

6# FEEL THE PASSION

Shivani wouldn't have done anything with football if her passion wouldn't have asked her to. Passion plays an important role in one's life. And if one will pursue it, then it leads the steps to success. But not all get chance to take up their passion. Some don't even realize it, some do but are confused, some know but don't follow it. Passion also has some hurdles in between. When Shivani told her parents that she wanted to pursue her passion with football her parents shouted on her. In fact her father slapped her, but she kept on arguing. Her family was a religious one, they saw football a sports established for men. The only person who supported her to achieve her dream was her best friend

Bhawna. Shivani very well knew that it was not easy to be a great footballer especially in India where football didn't had scope and she didn't had enough money to settle down in abroad. Despite of all the dark clouds she didn't lost hope and waited for the bright sun to come.

7# GERMANY

Shivani's hopes, hard work and talent made her fly to Germany, Europe. A football association from England visited India. They wanted to spread awareness about football and establish their branch in India. They had decided to select players, from a team and take them to England for a match. Almost they were three groups of selection and four rounds to be passed. Shivani was not able to take part in the selections as the auditions were for the boys. She asked them a lot but they could not change their orders just for her.

It was a regular day and she was doing her warm up when she saw a notice, it was the first notice she had ever seen on that notice board. It said the coaching organization is taking part in an international tournament and twenty five students will be selected from all over India. In the notice there was no particular gender mentioned so to confirm it she asked the head about it. He said that there are no barriers related to gender, there would be two teams one for the girls and the other for the boys. It was a great opportunity for her. There were almost six thousand children from across India. It was tough to get selected. Her parents didn't knew that she appeared for the auditions. When the parcel of Indian jersey and Reebok shoes came to her house, they were in a state of being speechless. Her mother was happy that she was selected. But they both thought that she was a kid and she cannot live alone without them. She was seventeen years old that time! Shivani was asked to forget about this tournament. She had worked so hard for this day, how could she just throw all her dreams out of her mind so easily. She left a note in her room and departed for the tournament. She even took some money out of her mother's bag. She then took the flight to Frankfurt along with other children and her coach. Shivani flew up high to fulfill all her dreams and was successful. It was not easy to compete with big teams like England, France, Brazil, Germany and Poland. India did not occupy the first or the second position instead got the fourth rank but the tournament marked Shivani's beginning. Though it's a totally different story that after coming back to India she was awarded with slaps from her parents.

8# LATER TALK

After the tournament she was offered sponsored coaching. A rich man from one of the football organizations of Berlin offered Shivani a deal. He would pay all her cost including living, coaching and other facilities. However, transportation cost was not included. On the other way deal said that Shivani would join his football team after completing her skills. Shivani's Family didn't agree on this neither she had the money to run from the house and catch the flight for Berlin. But this did not meant the end for her. One of our classmate told her about a very successful and a rich person. After that Shivani was lost from the school. No one except her best friend tried to contact her. One year passed and there was no clue of her. There were many rumors about her during those days. Children said, she would have been asked by the school to get out, she would be suffering from illness or may be her parents no more wanted to waste their money on her. Neither of these were true. She was working on her football skills. The person whose contact number our class fellow gave was also a retired footballer. He helped Shivani to improve her weak points. She also represented India in Asian Football Championship.

9# SECRET !

When we had the reunion of our class there used to be talks about Shivani. Some said that she will soon make her debut as the captain of our women football team and represent our country. Where as some said she is dead. Both had no proof so it was very difficult to believe one. The class fellow who gave her that contact number had no idea about her and her best friend never opened her mouth. Once, I went to the hospital with my mother. We both were waiting for our turn. There were six more patients before us.

I was busy with my phone and my mother said "I have seen her somewhere."

She pointed to a weird working girl sitting on a wheelchair of twenty six and coming out of the doctor's room. My mind said the same thing as my mother's mind. However, I could not recognize her. Holding her on the wheelchair was a famous footballer, Raman raj. I could not resist and asked him for his autograph. He gave me with a smile. But I could see that his smile was fake.

When he was giving me his autograph, the weird looking girl looked at me and said "Oh! My God."

I had no idea what she really wanted to say.

Raman bent down to her and asked "What? do you need something."

She replied humbly "No."

And they walked away. After two days I saw a friend request from a girl. I opened my facebook account and checked. The girl in the picture was the same weird looking girl I met in the hospital and the name read Shivani. I thought that this girl would be the same Shivani I knew in my schooldays but how could she turn being so ugly. The Shivani I knew was a very good sports person how could her activeness end up in a wheelchair. So I dropped my thought. Then I searched about Raman Raj. And the conclusion to my research work was shaking. Shivani was his wife. My mouth was left open. It was confirmed that the weird looking Shivani was the same Shivani I knew. I asked her best friend to arrange a meeting with her. After many requests she agreed. And then there came the day when I met her. She was no longer beautiful and had lost all her grace. I asked her the reason behind her wheelchair. She hesitated, but then patiently narrated her sad story.

Shivani had just started her journey as a footballer. Raman and she were in the same football coaching. Raman had fallen in love with Shivani. She always asked him to settle first and then think of love and marriage. He did not wanted to agree but he had to. Shivani and her group of girls were practicing when one of the girl came into anger. In anger she cost her temper and threw the ball towards Shivani with lots of force. Shivani tried to control the ball and lost her ankle. Her right ankle was permanently damaged. All her dreams shattered into pieces. That time when she had no one around Raman helped her. He married her and is getting her treatment done. It's not she will be able to play football again but she will be able to walk. She is getting her ankle replacement done.

10# HAPPY ENDING

Shivani would have lost her age. But her spirit and passion was not lost. She and Raman started a football coaching center for girls. India will succeed with football. Her family realized what her real talent was. All their scolding's were proved wrong. She was sent to earth to support every girl who admires to be a footballer. Her best friend Bhawna is also very successful. Shivani still fulfills the needed formalities for her and Bhawna's friendship. Raman lives Shivani's dream. He does his best to keep her happy. They both no more feel upset about Shivani's ankle. All the teachers mention her name to the students in our school. At last as usual I inspire her.

Approaching The Sky

1# Introduction

My face would not be the most beautiful one but yes my heart is! I am Rani, the queen of my life. My life may not be the simplest one but it's also not the most complicated. I live in a joint family and my family has eleven members. Dada, Dadi (my grandparents) Bade papa, Badi mummy (my father's brother and his wife), Mom, Dad my parents and my Chachu (My father's younger brother) and four children my elder sisters Sumi and Pari, me and then my younger brother Aditya. Interesting thing was that neither my mother and dadi ever had a fight nor did my badi mummy. Aditya was a big headache for me and he was a pampered child and also the most loved one, being the youngest in our house.

2# Teenage Living

On my 13th birthday my relatives wished me "Happy Birthday Teenager". I could not find anything different on that day. It was the same as my all passed 12 birthdays. I just got a tag of being a teenager. After some time I started realizing what was teenage. Changes in my body, changes in my thinking and development in my attitude, friendship getting more important to my life and being in the need of attention. Feeling was to be in the lime light always. Surrounded by my friends was my forever wish. On the other side I also prayed for my better and good marks, I ensured god that I didn't pray only for my benefit and asked him whether he was fine or not.

3# AIR HOSTESS

I loved travelling in an aircraft. When we used to travel abroad my excitement was more for sitting in a plane than travelling abroad. And whenever I travelled in an aircraft I used to start a conversation with the crew in the aircraft. I enjoyed talking to them. When the aircraft took off and when it landed my ears went through a buzz sound of feeling. So I carried bubble-gums with me but the problem came was where to throw it. I did not wanted to keep it with me the whole way so I threw it under my front seat. After doing this in the end when the aircraft landed I said sorry to the crew if I had done anything wrong. When I was asked by people what do I want to become when I grow up my answer would always be an airhostess as I will get a chance to travel all across the globe and interact with all sought of people.

But my parents said "If you want to fly then take the pilot job not an air hostess".

4# BEING PROFESSIONAL

Choosing a profession is really a tough job. I had no idea I would be so confused while filling my stream option form.

Whenever I question someone on which profession I should choose the reply was "Its your choice follow your interest."

I thought that interest will develop in any of the field if you want to develop it. Bade papa said go for teaching, dad said follow my business.

And mom joked "You wanted to be an air hostess, but go for pilot. And then we can move free around the world."

Last answer which chachu gave was a doctor. I used to get attracted to the white a doctor wears and the 'Dr.' term attached to your name as a prefix is amazing; on the other hand the cap with Indian flag brooch and a nice white and blue color suit that a pilot wears is superb. Final decision was to take science. Pari di told me that science will lead the way to all the professions. She asked me to do well in class eleventh and twelfth, score good marks and then give the thought on a particular profession. Sumi di thought differently, she asked me to go being a pilot. As I always wanted to be on clouds. I was totally confused on what to do. Then after hundreds of thoughts I decided to go with the pilot idea.

5# CRASH

All was well. My first semester had just ended with a lot of relaxation I took the newspaper in my hand after a month (I guess due to my exams. I stopped reading them). 'The 'Fly high airlines' crashed with 352 people on broad.' The headline read. My face in shock and mouth with exclamation said 352! I read the whole article. The conclusion was that the airline fly high Boeing 778 had departed from Taupe, New Zealand and was scheduled to arrive in Sydney, Australia. But according to the reports, it was missing after 40 minutes from departure. The airline lost all its contact with the center. The head department doubted it may be in the Pacific Ocean. I felt the story was very touching as the paper said that possibility of survivors (14 crew members and 338 passengers) is very dark. Immediately after reading the story I reached the two mentioned destinations in the atlas. I was doubtful that it was an accident or a suicide by the pilot, because last year there were two more crashes in which one of them was a suicide. Ironically the same airlines crashed last year too. My search said that the plane is in Tasman Sea, which is between New Zealand and Australia. It could had been in Pacific Ocean but the ocean was not on the flight's route map. Last location tracked of the airlines was near the Tasman sea, so there was a possibility of airlines floating on the sea. Being an active citizen I mailed my information to the newspaper office and asked them to print it the next day, as I had no idea how to contact the head of airline. The head of research work may have read my opinion and ordered search in that area. After one week I stood, holding newspaper in my hand and tears in my eyes. My research work was right; the plane had crashed in the Tasman sea. But the sad part was that there were no survivors.

6# PILOT

My confusion had mixed up with the air after the incident. And then my mind said "I know what to do in my life." My aim now was to be a pilot. Almost half of the population of world knows that there are many cases where either the plane goes missing or it is hijacked. But people don't stop travelling, so how could I stop dreaming the dream of becoming a pilot. According to the internet there was a short list of criteria's to join the airways. I would had loved to go in air force, as I'll do something for my country and die peaceful a death with fame. But my parents gave a yes to pilot after so many 'please!' I needed lots of guts for the permission of a pilot in the Indian Air Force. I had already made sacrifices to fulfill the dream of a pilot. I had to fix television hours and I could only use the phone for ten minutes. Which simply meant no more movies and entertainment.

7# LONDON WAITING FOR ME

I got 92% in my twelfth bored examination. According to me they were the best marks I had ever got. My parents were really proud of me. They could not believe that I scored ninety percent in twelfth. My dadi after hearing the results marked a black dot on my face (Kala Teeka) to protect me from the evil eyes of people. Pari di and chachu organized a party for all my close friends and our relatives. It was the first time when my friends were going to visit my home. I was extremely thankful to them, as they both were the reason behind my friend's visit. The party was amazingly brilliant. The next problem came when I applied for institutes. Even though not so many people take pilot as a profession still the cut off was very high. It was above 95%. Hearing this my house went in a silent cave. I blamed myself saying how could I just leave 3%. So I decided to try out universities in abroad. Amsterdam, London and Berlin had the best universities for the course of a pilot. I cleared exams with good marks not as good as a topper but yes good marks to get admission in a university of London. My joy had no limit. My family opposed my decision for London, but my sisters managed to convince them. I was the first one from the family to study abroad. Finally the time came when I had to take my flight for London.

"I wish I had a reason to stop you Rani." Said my mother with bundles of tears.

I hugged Pari di so tightly that she says for the next two days she had pain in her shoulders. Then, carrying lots of clothes and medicines I departed with memories. London welcomed me with open arms. My university was unimaginable. The way from my hostel to the university meant a ten minute walk. Starting from the building it was a five floor building with ten rooms per floor except the ground and the top floor. The room was a combination of pink and light blue on the four walls. The top wall was in white and the floor was tiled in cream color tiles. My professors were mainly male's and there was only one female professor. The boys said they all wanted to be with her forever. She was very beautiful. Coming to my hostel, it was a nice place bounded by lots of greenery. All the students were very well dressed up. I really admire their dressing sense. There were fixed timings for breakfast, lunch and dinner. Set up accordingly with the institute timings. Big Ben stood proudly on my way to the institute from my hostel and every day I clicked a photo with Big Ben and mailed it to my younger brother Aditya. Time passed mainly years passed and on my last day in the hostel, me and my batch was asked to plant a plant or maybe a tree with a tag of our names.

8# Air India

I was back to India after my education, I had completed and holded a degree with the permission to fly high above the clouds. I joined Air India. When I was approaching for my test I could not resist myself seeing down from the top while flying the plane. And as a result I passed the test with grade B. On the second level, I flew the plane high with confidence and again passed. First day, first trip and first flight. My nervousness was above my excitement. While starting the engine my mind said "remember the god first, you fool !" I took god's name and started the journey. "It's a safe landing," I repeated twice and saw the confused faces of other crew members present inside the airline as they must name thought that I was mad. I cannot tell and describe the feeling when I wore that pilot dress costume.

9# Co- Pilot

I was offered a tour of six days and two flights. It was my first tour as a pilot. At the airport I was introduced to my co pilot. His name was Vicky Singh. He was handsome! Our first trip was from Delhi to Chicago, non-stop and so many hours.

We were in the cabin and he said "let's put the plane in the auto mode."

I questioned myself that does he want to talk to me. I didn't wanted to say no, but I had to, as I was on work.

"If you are feeling tired, I'll drive and you can rest."

He knew that I had indirectly refused.

"No, its ok!!"

I was happy about his decision. And we safely landed in Chicago. It was the beginning of our second trip, which was from Chicago to Paris. The journey started well, but with time it became worst and in the end it was safe. We were on our way. I went to use the washroom, when I came back to the cabin he was in full stress, complaining about the controls. He said the control button is not working. I panicked. Announcement was made in the airlines to tie up the seat belts. People prayed and their prayers worked, we managed the controls. After the plane landed safely Vicky came to me saying

"Thank You so much for helping me otherwise I would have been blamed for the crash."

"No need for thanks, it was my duty."

We walked together out of the airport and all the eyes of people who came to pick up their relatives were at us.

He read my mind and said "It's ok the people respect us as we are pilots, they think of us as very important people."

From Paris to Delhi we travelled being passengers in an Air India airline.

10# Happy Ending

It was 5.00 am in the morning when I received a call from Vicky.

The call said "there is workshop and I have suggested your name for it. I will be waiting for you at 7.00 am at DDR."

DDR was a runway used by the junior pilots for practicing. He did not gave me the time to refuse or even to say a word.

I could not believe my eyes when I went to DDR. At the gate the board read "Welcome Rani"

With questions in my heart I entered the gate. There was a guide who told me that the workshop is inside that private jet. I walked in and there was complete silence. I could not see any faces.

Suddenly sound came "Welcome".

He came in holding a bunch of flowers and a dazzling smile on his face. As he came towards me and bent on his knees and said "will you marry me?" I had no reason to say no but many reasons to say yes. My answer went "I would love to. But I need the permission of my family and even your family."

"When we both were back from our trip, my parents came to pick me up they saw you and approved of you. My parents are coming to your house for the proposal. You just tell me that are you interested or not. He said in a sweet caring voice."

I took the bunch of red roses and smiled showing my teeth. He was filled with happiness. He took me to a helicopter, as soon as we sat in and tied our belts the helicopter departed. He gave me a bag like structure to wear. He opened the door and we jumped out of the helicopter into the sky. The bag was a parachute.

Today is my marriage with Vicky. I am happy that it's also an arrange marriage. His family is very social and broadminded. They have no objection with me being a working wife. I hope for the best with many more dreams of mine.

A Shoulder To
live - Friend

1# Introduction

She is not just my Mother's friend's daughter but more than
a best friend to me. Our first meeting didn't went the way I
assumed, but still today we eat, sit, dance and live together.
It was raining outside the campus. She held a cup of hot tea
in her hands, just brought from the canteen. I slipped due
to the rain and while she did a try to save me, the cup of hot
tea spilled over her. I could not do anything.

"I am sorry!" she said in her calm voice.

"No, actually it was my fault." I said.

We quarreled on the silly topic of whose mistake it was. We
were in Kerala in the same college. Our mothers were school
friends, who got connected after so many years. They asked
both of us to meet each other. We stopped the quarrel and
visited the infirmary. I am Tanya and she is Radhika. We are
often called Tanu and Radha. This was how our story began.

2# A BED OF FRIENDSHIP.

Whenever we met usually it was raining. After the incident we became best friends. It was not that we didn't had any friends before but yes we didn't had a friendship like ours before. We were in a hostel in Kerala. We bunked the classes together, danced in the rain together, slept under the sky together and cheated in exams together. We were both the same and often wondered that we should had been born sisters. There existed a bond between us which was similar to the bond between a plant and sunlight. Plant requires sunlight for survival and I was dependent on her. There were students jealous of me and her. Chaya, One of our classmate who tried to built a wall between our hearts. She said to Radha that I complained about Radha behind her back and often asked people to stay away from her. Chaya said the same thing to me. Due to the connectivity of our hearts through our souls, we found her guilty. We wanted to throw her in a burning volcano so that she burns in the flames of jealousy. Next day we didn't even looked at her. Radha was very pretty. She had a long list of boys behind her. She won the Beauty contest twice. We both did not needed anyone in our lives.

3# SYMPTOMS TO DEADLINE

Radha and I were working together on a project.

We were in the Library and suddenly Radha said "I think my stomach is not well. Sounds are coming from inside. I guess the food has made something go wrong. I had told you that there are news's of Pappu's food being stale and you didn't gave a damn."

"Okay! Fine I am sorry, do you want to visit a doctor?"

There was no reply from her side but I could see that she was not feeling well. We went back to the class as there was an important lecture.

She again said "It's getting over now."

I thought she was talking about the time left for this period to get over. So I kept quite with my eyes on the board she stood up and as she stood up she vomited. Everyone looked at her with weird expression on their faces.

"It's okay. Be patient go to the washroom." I said patting at her back. Everyone looked at both of us as if we were not humans.

After two days of complete rest she came to me with fears. I thought that we are meeting after two days so she will be coming with lots of stuff to share with me. She had lots of stuff to share but along with her fears. She complained that in two days she had experienced a mixture of illness, loss of appetite, painful urination, vomiting and sever cramps. She had gone through the web and couldn't find a reason behind all this. It was clear that all this didn't happen because of Pappu's chat that we had the day before the incident. I listened to her and then called her mother. She said she will be coming to Kerala in a day's time. Next day Radhika's parents arrived.

Her mother's first reaction after giving a hug to Radha was, "Oh my god! Why are you so hot!".

"We are like this always!". I said.

"No, Tanya she is hot. Really her temperature is too high."

When we checked her body temperature, it was 102 *Celsius*.

4# CANCER?

Our exams had to start within some days. I had to prepare for exams so I didn't visit the doctor with Radhika and her parents. I was so deeply involved in my studies that I didn't hear a knock twice. At the third knock I opened the door. It was Chaya.

I asked her "What the hell are you doing here?"

"I have no craze for you and your room. I am just here to inform you that Radhika is in a serious trouble. She is not well. She is back from visiting the doctor and is crying since then."

I had nothing to say back to Chaya. I wore my sleepers and ran towards Radha's room. She was lying on her bed crying.

Her mother was saying a prayer of lord Ganesha. And I was trying to figure out the reason behind all this.

Her father entered the room and said "Oh Tanya! Thank God you are here. Now, please stop your friend from crying. To make tears go ut of your body is not at all a solution."

I started making efforts to stop Radhika but she didn't stop her tears. I asked her mother "what all had the doctor said?"

I couldn't believe my ears. The doctor had told them that the symptoms faced by Radha were similar to the symptoms of cancer. He had also told them that he is not sure. It is yet to be confirmed through biopsy.

"So don't panic just pray its not." I urged.

Radha's biopsy test would be done the day after tomorrow. Biopsy is the only way to detect cancer. I hate the sentence that came out of my mouth during the discussion which simply lead to more tears in Radha's eyes. The sentence was 'Then she'll also not be able to appear for exams.'

Her father called me out of the room and said "You have your exam the next day, you should go and study. When we were coming back to the hostel from the parking, I had told Chaya not to inform you as you would be distracted from your studies."

I knew there was something fishy behind Chaya telling me about Radha as if she cares for both of us. Next day my exam went worse as hell. Chaya was successful in her plan.

Writing answer for every question I could just see Radha in tears.

5# SHATTERED LIFE

Biopsy is the only way to make a definitive diagnosis of cancer. Biopsy is the removal of a small amount of tissue for examination under a microscope. Radhika had gone through this. All of us saw her suffering. She had been detected suffering from cancer or a carcinoid tumor of appendix. It usually occurs when cells in the appendix become abnormal and multiply without control. These cells form a growth of tissue, called a tumor. A tumor can be cancerous or benign. For a carcinoid tumor of appendix the average age at diagnosis is about forty. It is rare in children and adults. But it is in Radhika's body for sure. She was suffering from cancer. It was at the first stage, so it could be recovered or cured. The doctor had warned her that the cancer would be soon moving to second stage. First stage includes the size of tumor being 2 cm or smaller, the tumor directly invades the abdominal wall or other near by organs. The primary tumor can't be evaluated.

6# THANK GOD !

Our exams were over. The Result which came out was very pleasant and according to our minds. I was one of the toppers in the list. My first exam had got me 69 marks out of 100. I feared that I will get fail in that exam, but I passed with good marks. On the result day I realized that the saying 'people who dig hole for others get caught in that themselves' is true. Chaya who wanted me to fail, herself became a failure. She had failed in three subjects out of five.

After six months Radha was in a better state, both physically and mentally. As soon she felt her recovery she applied an application asking permission of re-exams for her. Our dean approved the application. But she had to wait, she will be a part of final exams held for the children who were our juniors and present seniors of the college. While I had applied for admission in SK University, Rajasthan for my further studies. Radhika utilized the time given to her. She worked hard on her studies and she was the topper who got the highest rank which is Rank 1. She was sure that in any state of India, she will get admission in any college. And she applied in my college. The only thing sad was that she was my junior. I joined the college before her. Still I would thank god for everything I and Radhika got as a gift from them (gods).

7# Still Holding Hands

It was the fresher's party organized by my classmates and obviously me. I was again filled with jealousy as the 'miss beautiful girl SK' in junior batch was won by Radhika. She was again one of the most beautiful girls present in the college. She also won best dress up for her black shining silk gown with white beads. It didn't matter to both of us that we are not of the same batch. Our habits were still the same. I didn't had anyone in my batch as my friend. Radhika often felt upset about numerous rumors about us and specially me. Being a junior she could not answer them back and I had on one to support me when I answer them back and start an argument.

8# THAT WHITE GIRL

Time passed and passed. From the fresher's party till that day, we both were happily living two lives. Radhika being my junior had organized my farewell. The party was organized very well. Flowers were decorated all around. I was given a bouquet of pink roses and yellow lily's. My favorite! After the party there was evening tea and dinner too. I and Radhika ate food in the same plate. Our exams went well and the result automatically went well. This time instead Radha I was the topper. She took the second position in her class. My batch mates and I were given two days to check out of the hostel and get back home. In two days Radha and I wanted to live every moment as then we will not be able to meet. Radha will be completing her studies and I will be working in a company or doing any other job.

Next day of our result we would got a week's holiday. So we both visited Jaipur. In Jaipur we stayed in a five-star hotel. In the same hotel there was a tourist (white girl) living next to our room. During the breakfast Radha took the last bread piece left. She wanted to take it but Radhha was before her so she took it. The same situation happened with the taxi.

We took the hotel taxi before her. Though these things were not so big to build a issue but she did and saw us as enemies.

When we arrived back at the hotel after visiting Amer Fort (A Historical Place in Jaipur). I went to my room and Radha was at the reception. Our room's door was open. On besides my bed a nice tidy envelope was placed. I opened it and read.

The envelope said "I am like your friend. You may not like my letter but it is true. Your friend Radha is going to kill you one day. She is your enemy. Don't believe her sparkling eyes and innocent face. I know the importance of a friend, but a person having a foe in her heart cannot be a friend. I also know that you won't believe me and trust me, with time you will yourself see the truth coming out in Radha's actions. Don't close your eyes and believe in Radha. If you do, you will close your eyes forever."

I crushed the paper and threw it on the floor, under my bed. I didn't asked anything from Radha, I thought she will feel really bad and think that I don't trust her. I was not able to sleep the whole night. It was 2.00 am in the morning I got off the bed, checked whether Radhika was sleeping or not, took out the letter and read it again. After reading it. I packed it back in an envelope and placed it along my earings inside my bag. The same day when I and Radhika went down for lunch. She told me that she has an urgent call to attend.

Within next few minutes a waiter with a covered dish came and placed it on my table saying "Radhika ma'am has ordered this for you."

I opened it, it was a crab, a dead body of a crab. She very well knew I was pure vegetarian then how could she order a crab as my lunch. I stood up and went back to my room. Radhika came into the room searching me.

I just said to her "I cannot believe this, how could you do this to me. Why are you doing this?"

She couldn't understand what I was saying she kept me asking what her mistake was but I didn't gave any reply to her. Next day when we were checking out of the hotel I received a call which was from an unknown number. So I didn't pick it up.

In the same minute I received a message stating "I had informed you before hand about all the stuff. I think by now you would be knowing the truth. With wishes, your well wisher."

I searched the number from which the message came. It was from one of the rooms of the same hotel.

We were back to our hostel and I immediately packed my stuff took a taxi and left for the railway station. I took the first train to Guwahati.

My mother opened the door and the first question she asked me was "What happened between two of you? You didn't even greeted Radhika before leaving".

The answer from my side was "Please let me live in silence."

When I told her every part of truth, she felt exactly same as me.

9# NOT AGAIN

It had been four years since Radha and I met. During this time we remembered every memory we shared but didn't contact each other. One day I was on a off from my job when a postman with a letter came. Letter was from Radhika. "Please Reply. It has been four years today and you have not given a reply to any of my letters". This was the first letter I had received from her, but she had mentioned 'any letter'". My mind went puzzled out. I asked the post office head about the letters. He gave me a sheet of all the letters delivered to my house in past four years. There were around twenty eight letters from Radhika. The sheet had my mother's signature. I ran home with full speed. With anger I questioned my mother. She went to her room and bought a packet full of letters. She said "here are all, I haven't opened any of them. I kept them hidden from you as you would have felt bad. I opened the packet and patiently read all the letters. The letters said, she is unknown of the reason for which I didn't did a talk with her in Jaipur, she feels sorry if she was wrong some where in our friendship, she topped in the final exams and she received a call from a young girl who said her that she is a well wisher of her and asked her not to trust me, when we were back from Jaipur to hostel Radha found a letter which had exactly same things written in which I had received in Jaipur. She also mentioned the number of that well wisher. It was same the number as my well wisher. One thing was clear that a person mainly a girl who also was in the same hotel was trying to create a misunderstanding between us. When I reseached on this topic (It almost took one month). I found out who was behind all this. According to my research work, experience, reality and hotel staff the girl behind this was the white girl, the tourist which was next to our room. She had been spotted visiting our room thrice on that day, when I read that letter. She did this as we born insulted her in front of the hotel staff and because she saw us as her enemy. One of Radha's letter included a Photo of her being bald with a statement "My new hairstyle" it also included "I am sorry, my loving sister. Please come back in my Life. I am again moving along to deadline." I couldn't understand anything, the letter had the title – **NOT AGAIN**. When I had a talk with my mother about the letter she informed me that Radhika is again witnessing the symptoms of cancer. Cancer did not leave her completely. And now it is at fourth stage. This letter was written when her cancer was at third stage. I felt so sad, she did not wanted to put me in a state of stress so she didn't informed me. By now her tumor had spread into her body parts. It will be removed, mainly cells would be removed. But it is not that if the cells are removed the cancer is also. Doctors didn't had hope for her survival. The possibility was less. I came to know all this when I called Radhika's landline. Her brother picked it up and informed me they are in New Delhi for her treatment. I had a feeling to jump from Guwahati to Delhi in one go. My heart also said the same thing as Radha's letter **NOT AGAIN**.

10# HAPPY ENDING

Today I am sitting next to her and writing this story. She cannot feel my presence as she has been forced by the injection to sleep. I thought whenever I'll meet her I will greet her with cakes, chocolates, smiles and a sorry. But now I was just allowed for flowers and tears. We were alone in the hospital, room no-17 and silence was speaking more than our voices. I wanted to say her sorry, I wanted to make her like the old Radha, I wanted to laugh with her, but I could not. The nurse enters the room and instructs me that a checkup has to be done so I need to get out. I obeyed the order, went out and cried with her parents. My tears had no control. The doctor came out of the room and informed us that she is out of danger but needs special care. My tears were wiped out by a single sentence - 'She will be fine in a month's time' (according to the Doctor). I could not stop thanking god, not for giving Radha a second life, but also for giving one more chance to our friendship.

TRACES OF BURN

1# INTRODUCTION

My life has made me realize that we should not lose hope even in the darkest time, we should not leave our dreams and we should always trust ourselves. Learn to forgive and forget for a better life. When god can forgive us for our mistakes, why can't we humans forgive each other. Forget things that makes you upset they don't deserve your precious time. Enjoy every moment, may be you leave the world tomorrow. No matter if you are not pretty still look at the mirror and smile.

I had never imagined I will not have one eye, though I had both the eyes when I was born. Time will change, your body will change, so will your luck but don't let your dreams change. I am not from a family with a very strong background. My parents always supported me. In my school days, I had friends whom I thought my world but when I had to go through fire no one came to rescue me. It's not I didn't had true friends. Shaira was my best friend and because of me she experienced sparks of fire. Vani was not the closest friend but when I needed her she stood beside me. I am Kaamna, the best person I know! In my life even when I was right I had to face bad consequences.

According to a website the number of women going through the same accident would range from 100 to 500 per annum. I wanted to share my story with you all. I hope you also learn from my life and those who have gone though the same story would get encouraged.

2# My Feeling

If god would have asked me to choose my gender. I would have told him male. Being a girl simply means being emotional, soft hearted, forgiving, bold, working all the time and not expecting praise for that work. We girls have to face so many problems from our birth till the age we die. Though situations are still better now, earlier we were killed before being born. Girls have to face discrimination also. Boys are permitted to leave anywhere they want, but we are questioned first and then it depends that will we get the permission or not, there is nobody to check what boys are wearing, but we have limits. Girls have to go through physical changes too. People expect a girl should know household as well as she should be educated. Why are these qualities not looked in men? It is said that the respect of a family is in the hands of a girl or a women of that family, why not a boy or a man of that family? Housewives are never praised for their twenty four hour service. But working men are praised for their eight hour job.

On the other hand we girls are made to help the world selflessly. God has given us lots of duties and pain but he will surely award us a better life than a boy.

3# GOD - THE BIGGEST KING

At some point of time in our life we blame the god for all the instances happening our lives. It's a true fact that we remember him only when we are trapped in some sought of trouble. I saw a couple visiting a temple every day. Soon I realized they just preach a statue of god not him. We all sometimes doubt his presence and lose faith on him. But believe me he follows us on our each stop, watching us. He will definitely punish the evils. Never lose faith on him, never lose believe on him and never doubt his presence. In my life there were too many moments when I felt that he is not there for me. And then I realized what happened was for my benefit. Life has made me realize that what he does to us, he does for our better future. Trust me, the day we realize what preaching god actually means we will live happily ever after.

4# COMMENTS

The whole life I have heard different types of comments. Every comment is captured in my heart. No matter sweet or sour. I was very good at my studies. Whenever I got my result, I had so many praises my way. Every third person gave me an encouraging comment. I know and agree that I am not as beautiful as any of the actresses, then why this world makes me realize that. My parents didn't gave me the permission to visit the parlor in my teens. Due to this I had to hear the stupid comments from my classmates. Some even said that I didn't had the money to visit a parlor. Like every girl I also got some cheap comments from idiotic people. I had a very loud voice and even in my class I could shout louder than the boys. My family usually gave me comments and asked me to speak softer. But I was born with this voice. I was not asked to choose a type of voice neither I had a button to low it down. At the end of the day these comments broke my heart. Bad comments were heard louder than the good ones. The stupid comments by stupid minds are a painful stress.

5# THE BURNING SENSATION

It was Autumn. I was in a botanical garden with my friends. Learning from the trees to let the bad things go from our lives. There was an ill cream parlor. We all were cracking jokes and talking, while waiting for our ice-creams. We heard our name been called and we took the delicious ice creams instead of a good amount of money. I was enjoying the taste of the delicious 'rastraw', a mixture of one scoop of raspberry and another of strawberry. It was my favorite ice-cream. Suddenly I heard the sound of a bike coming towards us in a very high speed. The bike had two men may be two adults riding. They took five rounds around us at high speed and then one round slowly. By this time we all had come to know that their intentions were not good for us. During the last round, the guy sitting behind took out something and threw on me. With me the liquid had also dropped on my best friend Shaira, on her right shoulders. We all panicked and they ran away. When it gave me a burning sensation, I realized it was ACID.

6# I Lost It

Rest of the girls took me and Shaira to the hospital. It was late as for few seconds we were shocked, then we panicked and then they called an ambulance. The ambulance also took same time as there was no hospital near the garden. I was admitted in an emergency room and Shaira was in the general ward. We both didn't had any idea what this acid could do to us. Our families were called and we could see them in a state of hypertension. Shaira's father's blood pressure became very low hearing the news. For the two bike riders the acid was just a liquid to harm us or may be me, but for us it was lot more than that. Shaira could no longer hear from her right ear, she had her shoulder with patches of burns and her hair had traces of acid. Where as I had lost my left eye completely and left side of my face was burnt. I was half blind. I was no longer pretty. Everything was finished for me and Shaira. There was only one thought in our minds- 'we will have to face discrimination the whole life'. The acid was a thief who stole our organs from us. We lost all our life in that one second.

7# MYSTERY RIDERS

None of us saw the faces of those bike riders as they wore helmets. I and Shaira had no guesses who they would be. While I was in the hospital Vani, who was present at the time of accident came to me.

"Do you know any guy who wears this watch or keeps this metro card with him?"

I was already very upset, so I didn't stressed my mind much thinking about a card or a watch and answered "No".

She left the watch and the card next to my hand saying "Maybe you are tensed and cannot recognize these, but the two riders are known to you. Take some rest, take your time and think, where have you seen these things. Get well soon."

The thought to kill both the riders was moving around my head. Then my hand picked that watch. I had seen it before in Shankar's hand. And his best friend Akshat always had a metro card with him, as he travelled by metro from school to his home. When I kept thinking I remembered that I was not in good terms with them. I called Vani and told her what I knew those two things about. She called the police and registered a complaint on my behalf. But, there was no response from their side for almost a month.

8# BLACK WORLD

The world looked at me and Shaira with grim expressions. They would show sympathy for us. We both were blamed for the burns we had. Even our families thought that we would be involved with them and as a reward they gave us these rashes. No one asked the true reason behind this. Shankar and Akshat were best friends and belonged to a very wealthy family. They were Shaira and my classmates. I was checking my notes with Shaira's notes.

Shankar came to me and said "This is the last year and you are already eighteen. So we can get married. My parents are ready. I'll come with them to your house and officially propose you." I stood up and gave him a slap. Akshat came and warned me for what I had done. I and Shaira walked back home.

The next day he came again and said "Still there is time. Think you will not get a husband better than me."

I was filled with anger.

I shouted loudly "Idiot! Don't you have a sister or a mother in your house. First learn how to talk to a girl. In such a huge population of India I will defiantly find a person better than you. And if I don't I'll still not marry you."

I could see that he was feeling insulted when the crowd saw us.

In that shame he twisted my hand tightly and said "You have not seen worst side of mine yet. So, now you will see it from all your six senses."

This all happened and after three days I found myself burnt. If I had agreed to marry him then also I would have been insure by my family and when I did what was correct then also I was blamed. Also, by this time Vani, Shaira and I had understood that the police was corrupted. They said that my identification of a match or a metro card can't be a proof against them and they had tried their best to catch them but they are not in this city. Vani insisted to fight against the police. I stopped her and asked her to file a case in the high court against the two black wolves.

9# STANDING AGAIN

It was tough for me and Shaira to face the world. For some time, we thought that we had lost our life and there was nothing left to do. Then Vani came as a magician and sparked her magic on us. She shared different success stories with us. Her stories made us learn that it hardly counts what you don't have, use what you have. Our family, our friends and faith on god made us realize that if we want we can still live our dreams. I wanted to stand up. The next problem that came was, because of the loss we had just faced. Nobody was willing to give us a job, despite of our degree. I was my parent's only child and the only hope for their better future. How could I let them down because of two mindless creatures. I decided to make the two wolves realize that nothing has changed in my life, I am not coward and I will not make myself upset because of them. I and Shaira started an NGO for acid attack survivors. We distributed pamphlets, advertised on television and used social media to spread awareness. In the first month we had only two girls as a part of our NGO and by six months we had around thirty girls. We all started a clothing business. Few went to buy cloth, few stitched them and the rest gave the final touch. We sold them to small shopkeepers and soon we started selling them online. In this business, we earned a good amount and divided equally. Our families were happy, our customers were happy and most importantly we all were happy. To stand again was not easy but I did it. Still somewhere in my heart I had the fear of falling again.

10# HAPPY ENDING

It's a true saying that 'if the end is not a happy one, then it's not yet the end.' After six years everything in my life is according to me and I love it. The court took the decision in my favor. Shankar and Akshat are in the prison. Shaira is happily married and is settled in Sikkim. Vani is a well known scuba driver, she never dreamt of being a scuba driver but with time she realized it. My NGO has twenty girls joining every year. The clothing business which I started is running very successfully. We are among the bestsellers online. Also, we have expanded the business in some European countries. After losing my precious one eye, I realized what the importance of our eyes is. Despite of the two wolves I am living in peace with my family.

THOUGHTS AND FAME

1# INTRODUCTION

My name is Kavya. I may be similar to many other girls but no one is exactly same as me. I am the one and only piece in the world. Everyone in this world is unique. I live in a house of four people, me, my parents and my sister Navya. Sometimes our lives are controlled by the people. We move and shape ourselves according to the society. People around us are jealous of us when we are higher than them, they don't see our efforts and struggle as jealousy makes them go blind. No one had guessed that I will be so much successful in my life. Despite so many problems I stand as a writer, a poet and a learner. I teach English in a school, 'Pathshala'. The school is very famous in Lucknow, my birthplace. My father shifted to Delhi for our better education. Like every successful person I also faced some problems.

2# FIRST POETRY

I was in class eight, I was upset thinking that in the next class I will not be with my friends as our classes would be shuffled. To express my sadness I wrote my first poem. Somewhere in my heart I knew I will no longer be happy as I'll be alone in the next class. Actually my first poem was not really a poem. It was just that I arranged sentences in a horizontal way and their last words would rhyme. My English teacher asked me to put in more efforts. My first and the second so called poem were all about sorrow in one's life. They explained situations of frustration and the wish to commit suicide. They touched many hearts.

3# AFTER EFFORTS

My poems may not be good, but my efforts were. Teachers supported me for my hidden talent, specially my English teacher. She taught me in class sixth and still helps me with my stuff. Almost half of my poems are edited by her. My class teacher, English teacher really encouraged me. My math's teacher used to ask me for my poems and read them with a smile; on the other hand my social science teacher got a list of publishers for me and every year for the school magazine she booked a space for my poems and articles. Two teachers who left the school and had taught me in my junior classes also appreciated my poems. My sister had to through them, expecting a reward for reading them. My friends were the all time support system for me. With the help of all these people in ten months I wrote about forty poems.

4# STORY - BEGINNING

I felt very disheartened when the people whom I considered my friends had turned into a foe. After getting hurt my heart wanted to jump out. For few seconds I sat on the back seat of my life. My frustration was unbearable. I took out my notepad and started writing a story of a girl who had numerous enemies. The day she learns, she is not ready to believe. This was my first story. My class mates and school fellows loved the stories and the youth enjoys reading it. Getting an 'ok' from people meant more confidence in myself to be a writer. After this I understood, luck is important to play a game, something's work on the first go and something's not even in the last. The irony was that my first poem was not a poem and my first story was not only a story.

5# FUTURE SELECTION

My parents didn't ask me any questions on the day my ninth class were out. They were not at all happy with the marks I scored 75%.

In the end they just said "Next time do your best or........"

At the start of tenth class I focused on my studies. Teachers gave me an applause for the great efforts I was making. It would feel brilliant to hear praise from them in front of the whole class. My tenth grades were far better from the ninth ones. I scored 89%.

"Good my daughter! I am proud of you" my father said with a laugh in between.

I had a strong writing power so I wanted to do literature honors. When I shared this suggestion with my parents their answer was unimaginable. They had straight away refused. They saw writing as my hobby. According to them I would not be successful in this. My mind said that the reason would be they have not read Shakespeare's work, Rabindranath Tagore or may be any great book. I knew my parents had their mind set up of eighteenth century but I would not say this on their face. Finally on the report card day when my teacher said it face to face they agreed. And when they were back home I was warned.

"If you are pursuing literature I don't want less than 90%." My father shouted.

6# SADNESS WITH FLAME

In my eyes whatever I wrote occupied the top position, but not in the eyes of other's. My teachers would encourage and appreciate me but my own family didn't. I used to hold Navya and force her to hear my poems. She didn't refused me but at the end of all poems she said "nice!". I knew from her actions and facial expressions that she heard them from one ear and dropped from the other. My parents never showed interest to what I was writing in the dairy. I asked them to read my stories and poems.

They didn't really read them and to keep my heart said "They all are equally good. We'll read the rest later."

There was no one to clap on my works. Sometimes I felt that people don't understand how amazing it is to write and read. My class mate Satwika regularly asked me if I had written any more poems. She read them and suggested me some changes. Children in my school treated me badly specially when I was shuffled in class eleventh.

I really had a wish to shout on them saying "Whom do you call beautiful, a girl with a clear face or a girl with a clear heart? What I don't have? How can you judge me? You are no one. I am also same as you. I may not have good looks, but take a look at my heart its more beautiful than yours. Talking about talent. I have written forty poems and many stories. What good have you done? Just showed off what you have or pretend what you are not."

I couldn't do it as my self - respect and loyal heart stopped me.

My friends who read romantic novels mainly love stories, one day came to me and said "You write good, it's a passion! Being your friend we would advise you that if you want to become a writer, a good writer you should move ahead from your comfort zone. Your writing style is very smooth. In these days people prefer love stories as youth is mainly interested in that. Some people may not like your way of writing. It's nice but we would advise you to write something on love."

For two seconds I could not reply them. But then my heart replied "Thank you for your advise. I cannot write love stories I know the youth will not like to read my stories, but it's not that I am writing them only for the youth. Parents will at least not think twice to buy my book for their kids. Even the old population will read it with joy. And it's not that everyone adult like love stories, some just hate love. Also, every writer has his own way of writing."

After all this, I was being underestimated. I wanted to burn my sadness into flames.

7# TO THE WORLD

I was all ready with my stories and poems. I now wanted to publish them. I tried so many publishes for my poems but there was no reply. I sent them my stories too. The reply was exactly the same as my friends said. The publishers complained that the world will not approve my stories as they were for kids. But they were not. They were about the life of people and I wanted people to learn that they are not the only ones struggling for happiness. I just wanted to increase their self confidence. When I went to a book shop I purchased five to six books about life. I also asked the shopkeeper about the demand of those books. He said many of them are bestsellers and are in a high demand. His last words made my heart relax. I read them all. I saw their publishers and contacted them for my stories. Two, out of four agreed and asked for further information. Finally my stories were published. I wrote my first love story, which was about my best friend's love story. It was a great love story. They both were best friends. She married him and are an ideal couple.

The people who never saw me and turned their back towards me and after recognizing me, they wished me and appreciated me. It was a tight slap to them and a relief to my self - respect. My stories were visible to the world. The people who questioned me and my qualities had to accept it. However, some people still took out mistakes in my work.

8# BACK TO SCHOOL

I was a well known writer, a poet and a painter. As soon as I was up with fame, I received a call from my school principle. She had invited me for a program organized for students of classes ninth to twelfth. The topic was success in life. I heard the topic and my heart just said that I could write thousand pages on this topic. I could not refuse her, though I knew I had no time and I was busy completing the final year of my literature honors.

I was welcomed at the school with lots of laughter, flowers and memories. They welcomed as if I had won a national award or I had just returned from a visit to space. The teachers asked me to include some topics such as how to achieve success, studies, passion, interests, distractions and confidence or self esteem in my speech. When, I was sitting on a comfortable chair on the stage. I saw the fresh faces of children showing they are least interested in my lecture. I knew their state of mind as I also passed the same school at the same age.

So, I started the speech "Don't worry you are not here to fight a war, don't be so serious. It's just an interaction program arranged for you."

And I saw smiles on their faces blooming up.

Later my speech included "Success is not something you can achieve so easily. It requires patience, confidence, hope, faith, love, support and of course hard work. It's not too tough to rise if you have self confidence in yourself. Always value your relations, specially your family who has supported you and who will always do. Never lose hope even in the darkest places of your life, because hope always lives inside you. Have faith in your surroundings. Love your family. To being in a relationship does not always means you are in love and happy. They are just waste of time. It's your life and you yourself are responsible for your joy and sorrow. It's not always that you marry a person with whom you were in a relationship before. When my class fellows asked me who is your valentine, my answer was my family. And I still remember them laughing on me. Stop being engaged in a relationship as they only make life complicated. Many of suicide cases have the reason 'RELATIONSHIP' behind. Be patient even in your fastest and worst times. Keep your mind cool, not with ice and cold water but with positivity and thoughts. Don't waste your time. Be sensitive to all.

Your emotions are very important. Discover your passion. Make your weakness your strength. Trust yourself first, not others. Always believe in yourself. Make your heart beautiful than your face. Prove people that you are not a looser, by making yourself successful not by shouting on them. Be kind, caring, truthful and rise the name of humanity."

After my speech I could see all the hands clapping. My heart felt relaxed as I won the hearts of children. At the end I interacted with the children and the teachers.

9# WORK FOR ALL

My life was one of the precious things I had. Success was all around me. My poems and stories were published. The audience waited for my next book, my paintings was placed along with the paintings of Johnny B.Ca, a worldwide famous painter at the painter's gallery. It was all no less than a dream come true for me. I was happy, my family was happy but still many people were not; Who thought they had been defeated by tears. I wanted to help them and continue the word 'help'. I went to villages gave them my Hindi version of 'sunrise'. It is one of my books, which includes some questions on life and what we should be. Even in the urban areas, I gave speeches. And then they delivered it to the helpless and broken heart people. My work helped many people. It also crossed many people. I was honored by the chief minister of Gujarat for my this achievement. My parents were proud of me, and this feeling made me go crazy.

10# HAPPY ENDING

My school, my family, my friends and Navya all were proud of me. I was just an ordinary girl. I am married to the chief minister of U.P. It was an arrange marriage. He lived in Lucknow so I had to shift back to my birthplace. I am in great joy. All that I have achieved in my life is a great example of passion towards success. Every person can write a story about his life if he wants to. We are born with a story. I have taken real stuff from my life and transformed them into a story.

In the end I would just say "Never run behind success, follow it. Never underestimate yourself, believe in yourself. The world is for all, let others live happily. Follow your passion. Never hurt someone as someday that 'someone' may be you."

UNDERSTANDING LIFE

1# INTRODUCTION

There are millions of people living on earth. Every person has a totally different life. All of us have problems, joy, sorrow and our own world. We go through tough times resulting in experience, which helps us to move forward in our life. And according to Shakespeare, we perform different roles in our lifetime. From the time we are born till the time we die, we experience life in infinite modes. We come with no money, no clothed and no name and we hug death the same way. We fear death, inspite knowing that we have to face it some day. I am Surbhi, a middle class girl, with multiple talents and a gorgeous smile. Just like all girls I also like to gossip a lot. I am gonna take you to a journey of some incidents that took place in my life at some point of time, leaving memories and only memories.

2# STILL NOT INDEPENDENCE

We all think that women are given equal treatment as men. We all think that there are no more marriages happening among children. Living in cities or may be in an outer world we don't realize what is going inside the inner side of world. I was in class tenth, when my history teacher told me one thing, a thing which gave an aim to my life. She told me that she had recently visited a government controlled school, located at the outskirts of a city. According to her there was not a single girl in a class of thirty students.

When asked the answer was "Girl? Why do girls and education, they need to study household to be a good housewife."

Thirty boys present in the class had almost same surname and seventeen of them had the same name. One thing was mirror clear that the area had a particular community living. Around fourteen of those boys were engaged, five had their marriage within a month and eight were already married. The boys were seventeen to eighteen years old and were forced to marry girls of age fourteen to fifteen. Though it's illegal to marry till the girl is eighteen. The government was not aware of all this non sense stuff or may be if they were this was being ignored. That day I realized that my country has still not achieved independence. Listening to my teacher gave me another dream. A dream where I make efforts to achieve gender equality.

3# A RAY OF HOPE

Whenever I am upset I lookout for an animal. Animals are much more intelligent than humans. They are hard working, united and they give back our love the same way. One day I saw a mouse in a cylindrical dustbin. The bin was almost empty, had some wrappers. It was easy to jump inside the bin but to get out was equally tough. I could see him making continuous effects to get out. He was not so tall to walk out from the cylindrical bin. Then a lady came with two packets of garbage and threw them into the bin. She walked away back to her home. When I kicked the bin, the mouse was absent, after giving some time to my mind I could understand that in the two packets he found staircase to get out of the bin. He must have climbed up the packets and ran out of the bin. He was much more patient than me. I didn't had so much of patience rather, I would had started shouting and making noises. A dog is a best friend, better than humans. Dogs are not selfish, they are kind. We humans bring them into our homes, we separate them from their families and still they love us. Ant is another great example of hard work. An ant keeps trying to move forward even when a human puts a barrier in-between. Birds and insects have better unity than us.

Animals are great examples to inspire.

4# THAT ONE FRIEND

We all have friends and enemies. In fact they both are present inside us too. I remember how my friends were my support to the way out from darkness. In my school days I had a group of five girls as my centre of laughs. One of my friend was a very egoistic person and at the same time a good friend with friendly attitude. It was Wednesday and the weather was very pleasant. I was waiting for her, outside her classroom. I could see anger in her eyes lines on her forehead and stress on her face as she walked in. I asked his several times what the problem was. The reply was nothing. Finally when she was irritated, she said that she will tell me after sometime. I thought she must have had a fight with someone or may be someone would have treated her badly, which would had hurt her ego. I also felt that she is keeping secrets from me, as I saw her instructing rest of my friends to shut up. I had started to form a bad image of her in my eyes.

Truth was totally different from my stupid thoughts. One of our class fellows had made a statement about me and my friend got to know the statement she was upset for me, she was angry for me and she was stressed for me. I was not a true friend of her's. How could I think like that. All her anger was clear when she made my class fellow stand still in silence. Her voice was heard clearly from one end of the corridor to the other. There were many instances with my same five jolly girls, which made me realize the importance of friendship. My friends made me learn what friendship is. We all have that one friend who is caring, sweet, truthful and honest. Value friends with time, as time does not stop and leaves us in a world of regrets and memories.

5# THE SWEEPING STORY

On a sunny morning I observed something that changed my mind. I got up a little early as I had plans for jogging. I stood outside in my balcony when my eyes were focused on a sweeper. There was dust running around him, also the bright sun was shining above his head. He had no concern to all this, his full attention was to the work he was doing. He received a phone call and I could understand from his words that it was urgent. He stopped his work, ran outside looking for a three wheeler. No one was ready. I went down asked him if I could give him a lift.

He said "No, I don't take favors ma'am."

I could understand his self respect but what about the phone call. After he received one more call, he changed his mind and in a respectful voice asked me if I could drop him. I dropped him near a flyover, I had to go ahead to take a U-turn. When I went forward I saw him hugging a child, wearing torn clothes. They both walked towards a hospital. I could see tears and fears in their eyes while walking. Inside the hospital, they had a conversation with a well dressed man and then they walked inside the room. It was a private hospital and I was speechless thinking that will the sweeper be able to pay the expenses for the person he is meeting inside the room. The story released afterwards was very sad. The patient and the other child whom he hugged are his grand children. The children lost their parents at a very early age. One of them, may be the elder one was the patient. They both work after attending the school. They supply grocery from market to the houses. By their way from the market the children were hit by a car. The elder one got a fracture, the younger one didn't got much hurt. The driver rushed him to the hospital, he was the one to call the sweeper first and the second call was from the younger kid. Hospital bills were paid by the driver as a punishment and regret. I had gone so deep into the life of that sweeper, that I wanted to dig more deeper. The next day was my holiday and I decided to research on the sweeper. I could only discover that he made every effort to bring a smile on the faces of his grand children. He was around sixty eight years old, he did not had lots of strength in his legs but he could match steps to a song when the children asked him to. Their house was a hut along with a construction site. Children used the sunlight to study. They made different kinds of art work with the torn and left over sticks, that too asking the sweeper twice. The sweeper worked so hard the whole day doing multitasking of jobs. All his tiredness disappeared when he saw one teeth dancing on the faces of his grandchildren. A small family with happiness. They realized that we have to accept life and its decisions for us. We cannot stop and wait for the conditions to improve. I learned a big to lesson from this sweeping story.

6# LIFE I MISS

No one of us remembers how we acted, how we irritated others, how we laughed, how we cried or in short how we were as a child. Life is always what we make it. We get choices for every decision we take. It's an option for everyone either to take situations in anger and live with a headache or take it lightly with a smile. We are always unhappy with our present life and so we spend lots and lots of time dreaming good future. When we lose something than we realize what it's value was. As a child of seventh standard I used to wish that I should directly move in a college, skipping classes in −between. I used to admire college life or high school life. My seniors used to walk freely, they had no tension of teachers on their head. Every time I stood in front of god, I just asked magic, I knew it was not possible, but still I would have asked the something from god more than fifty times. When I entered the world of high school, I saw a new phase of my life. I was no longer scared of my teachers in fact they were now just like my friend. I no longer wasted my prayers, praying for them to be absent. As I child we would party around when we got a substitution, but everything changed with high school. Now I used to be happy when I saw my teachers. As teenagers I thought friends are the most important people in my life. But with time I realized what my family means to me. And I missed my middle school days. There was no high pressure and huge amount of stress on my mind. During my middle school I dreamt about high school and college and when I was in high school I had a list of regrets for me. Just like me, we all are like this. We waste our time, destroy our present and dream about future. And then, we tell our past saying 'life I miss.'

7# REAL ART

Once I was walking on the roadside, with around six to seven shopping bags and I saw a seventy year old grey haired, long beard, two teeth and a weak man. He was painting a beautiful waterfall. He had already painted ten- eleven paintings, which were on sale. I stood there, holding my heavy bags, observing him and his hands, which were painting so fast that I could not even blink my eyes. He obtained the two teeth smile on his face while painting. His clothes were not branded, but his art was worth being called branded. His paintings were evolved around nature. One of those was a paintings which took all my attention. The painting had a little girl with a butterfly in her hand, behind her was a tree with pink and white flowers blooming. He observed me and started telling me the cost price for each painting. Form his expressions it looked that I was his first customer that day. I could not control and asked him some questions. He hadn't sold any of the paintings from almost a week. When he answered me with correct pronunciation of words I could see, he was a well educated man.

Again I asked him a question "You seem to be a well educated person, so why are you working as a painter. You can try out many other occupations."

I could feel sorrow in each word of his reply. "You are right my child, I have studied from one of the best schools of this city, but sometimes life holds you in a situation from where there is no way out. I had no other choice but to use and spread out my talent."

I was curious to know the reason behind this statement of his. This reason was a common one, among many old people. His son asked him to leave his house because of his wife. Also, his son refused to pay him an amount which could help the old person. With empty pockets, he was nothing. Somehow he managed to take a shelter and then start the painting business. With a soft voice he explained me that why and how painting, became an important aspect of his life. Being an artist he could see steps of life with reality. He explained me what really art is. Each of his work had a moral value along beauty. That day I understood how a real artist is created.

8# WHY?????

I had a friend Simi, she was one of my best friend. When I used to be with her I could understand all jokes which were cracked around me. She was a very cheerful girl and then no one could understand when that cheerful girl changed into a stupid girl. While our high school, we had extra classes. She was an average student, but then a failure. There was a gap, that had started to built between her and her parents. Firstly they forced her to do everything which she didn't wanted to and then blame all the matter on her head. She had started to have a very high blood pressure. She was never able to be happy again not even above the clouds (I guess!). She was ditched by her best friend. That girl broke her trust, which stood for over 5 years and gave her lifelong pain. Good marks meant it all for her parents, not good remarks. She thought every problem is related with her. And decided to end them up. Simi killed herself by jumping from a multi story building. She didn't had the guts to cut her nerve or overdose pills.

In her suicide note, she didn't mention any sentence but in the middle. "I am sorry."

The society forced her to do this. Her own people forced her. Why? Why did this happen her?

9# STRANGE VISITOR

When I was a teenager, I had a visitor coming in my house. That day my house looked like a new one. All preparations were made perfectly. I thought there would be someone special coming, so I asked my mother who is coming. She explained so many relations to me and I could just understand that the visitor was a relative of one of my family member. As preparations were never done this much neat. I thought the visitor was in good terms with us. But the reality was something different. The family person coming belongs to the family which was in bad terms with us. They think they are very rich, the best people anyone can know. My parents wanted to show them off our royalty. The visitor was a young girl of twenty two. She wore a printed floral dress and long earrings with open hair. She entered my house greeted my parents and hugged me, as if she knew me since past five years. She was not so pretty, but pretended like a miss world. Her hair were long and thick. Her stay was for six days but she extended it to ten days.

After she left my father said "She has troubled us so much, next week lets visit them."

I told him that it's not right. He didn't listened to me and said "You want to go on a holiday or not."

Who doesn't wants to go on a holiday that too in a hill station. I agreed and with this I also had to agree with my parent's stupid rules. They were telling me how to behave, how to talk, how to eat and how to sleep. I mean, I knew all these things from my childhood; what was the sense to tell me again and again. Then I realized their rules were to show the visitor's family how mannered I was.

We gave them a surprise visit. They were not at all good hosts. They didn't pay much attention to us, we gave their daughter a princess like treatment. I was so angry with this visit that I never wanted to visit that house again. However the place was very beautiful. We could feel the nature in that pleasant hill station.

I always wanted to have long hair but when I saw the visitor's hair all around in my washroom, I was happy with my hair. She was very strange and always complained about things. She was choosy and opted just for branded stuff. I came to know her, I could see the strange personality in her.

10# Happy Ending

If we do good, we achieve good. At the end, everything happens for a reason.

With time women are getting importance and equal rights. Women are realizing what they deserve. Animals are protected and many campaigns are being launched for them. We should realize the importance of true friendship. True friends are rarely found, value them. Respect them no matter what their profession is. The sweeper which I had talked about is still in the same situation but lives with more happiness. The old painter now has a showroom and is popular in the city. His paintings are sold every day. My friend Simi's parents realized what was the value of her life, after her death. They felt guilty on what they had done to her. Whenever, they see a parent forcing a child or scolding a child they ask them to be little softer and share their experience with them. After a visit to the strange visitors, my parents understood that we should not pretend to be what we are not. My family and I prepared ourselves very well but the hosts were least interested to treat us, talk to us or even greet us.

In life, experiences are necessary we learn so much from them. Stop fearing death, we know we can't stop it so why waste our life calculating the time left. Enjoy life it is given only once to live. Live in your presents without the regrets of past and the tension of future.

Disparity Of My Life

1# Introduction

My name is Kokum, I live in Kolkata and I study in a college doing my M-Tech. Talking about my present, it's just great. I am not the same as all. But like everyone I also have a past which is no less than a trip to hell. I may be one of the luckiest people that I stand today with a smile on my face but I was also one of the most unlucky people that I usually had tears on my face. I was never a topper and I am still not a topper. My creative skills always lead before my academic skills. I live in a nuclear family. Including my parents, it's me, my sister Cavite and my elder brother Kush. And the interesting part is that my family members have names starting with 'k'. I am going to tell you bits and chits of my past and parts of my present. Let's start with my past.

2# Twin Factor

One of the most important factor in my life is the twin factor. Cavite is my twin sister. We both have a difference of five point eight minutes in our birth. She is elder than me even though just five point eight minutes. She always cuts the cake first. From my attitude and did a talk with only those who had a standard. She was so active on facebook that almost 50% of the school was her friend and a fan too. In school whenever I asked Kush for anything he said "just go away. I am your brother at home not in the school. Don't insult me." Whereas when Kavita did the something as mine he smiled at her, even introduced her to his friends. This happened may be because I was not good looking, had an oily skin and did not survived in attitude, my heart was open for all. From childhood till now she is thought to be better than me in every field. She is beautiful than me and always had boys around. I was a very jolly nature girl. I used to shake hands with everyone does not matter the person had a poor or a rich status. She was filled with. No one listened my complaints about Kush. The partiality Kush did always made me feel lonely. I had no one to share the thoughts of my heart. I used to put my favorite soft toy, a teddy bear and 'bunny', in front of me and narrate my thinking to him. This made me a patient of mental illness in the eyes of my family. I knew he was not alive but he had two eyes, one nose and all the features we had as humans except voice and at least he did not gave me a cut in my heart. He was the best person in my life. Kavita and I stood for the school elections. I nominated my name first, but as she was friend of the previous captain her name was selected. After approaching teachers I nominated myself again but as usual she won, because of her popularity, attitude, beauty and fake friendship with people.

3# THE NAIL

I knew I was alone in the world but I used to make myself understand that I am not lonely. Incidents happened when I and Kavita used to study in class eleventh. She was the vice head girl of school. There were two incidents of nail that made me an enemy to the class. That year there was a new principle who took over our school, Mr. Bhalla, a retired cornel from the Indian army. He was very particular about everything related to school name. Kavita was a total diva. Even in the uniform she made herself look like a star, she had short socks, a short skirt, two rings, perfectly shaped nails, matching nail paint with the rings, a locket with her name, long earrings and a pony tail (hairstyle). When teachers asked her to stop wearing and doing these things she gave them an example of one of our seniors. But there was a person whose terror she felt. Sir, our principle, one day sir came to our class for a random uniform checking. I had my nails short with white hills on them indicating deficiency of a nutrient. Sir, passed and checked Kavita's uniform and nails but there was no complaint from him. I was sitting in front of her and next was my turn. He checked my long socks, nails, earrings. I thought there would be a positive reply from him praising me, as I was the only one in the class with oily hair, long socks and wooden earrings. Waiting for reply I with a smile looked at him.

He said "Don't you get time in your house to do this, do you wash clothes or dust the furniture? If you are doing something against the school then face it."

My mind could not remember what wrong had I done, so I kept quite. He called my class teacher.

Calling her, he said "look, look what is going inside your class."

Sir was showing her pieces of nails under my chair. Teacher asked me to pick them up.

He gave me a warning. "It is the first time so I am leaving you, but if next time I see this, I will take an action against you."

With time I came to know the mind behind the tragedy I had gone through. Kavita, being a council member knew about the checking. She took all her accessories out and bought a nail cutter and nail polish remover. Her best friend helped her cutting nails. And the same nails were lying under my chair.

The second incident happened on the farewell day we were dressed up in beautiful dresses and were prepared to give our seniors a memorable farewell. I was in the dance group and was ready to perform on two hit songs of Shahrukh Khan's hit films. Kavita and her group was handling the settings of the auditorium. Kavita was tightening the screw of the board which had to be placed on the stage but by mistake it got loose and the screw was in her hand. There was no time and she could not fix it again. So she left the screw opened in its place. My performance was first and I was standing behind all in the last row. The song began, I started with my steps and as I took a turn the board dropped on the stage hurting my leg, the wooden side of the board which was coming out gave me along black cut for lifetime. I was bleeding badly. I was not the only one, two more girls were injured we were given immediate aid. farewell, which I wanted to make memorable, was one of the most memorable days for our seniors but in the bad terms. School staff tried to catch the hand behind the misery. As Kavita and her and gang was responsible for the settings, they were questioned. They blamed Gopal bhaiya for all this. He had brought the board from the basement to the auditorium. He was not paid his one month salary. I felt so sad for him but I had my hands packed. It was nothing I could do for him.

4# EXAMINATION

Only two months were left for my eleventh class examination. I wrapped myself with all sought of books. I read them. Physics was really tough for me to achieve. So I used to make Bunny sit in front of me, take out the old black board and started teaching him like his physics teacher. In my class I saw Kavita making a new friend circle. Aisha topper of our class, she was a average looking girl with a fat body. She had friends, which were totally different from Kavita and her gang. Kavita was trying to impress Saurav, our classmate. He is intelligent and handsome too. Everyone knew something was going in the class. We could see that there was something going on inside Kavita's mind. She was trying to get involve with Aisha and Saurav. No one could understand her aim. Exams were within a week so I stopped thinking about the world. Kavita used to sit before me. Beside her was Saurav and Aisha. Kavita had notes, photocopied in small size kept inside her socks. She exchanged question papers from Saurav and Aisha. We had five exams, in every exam she cheated the same way and when we came out of the examination hall she thanked them with a 32 inch smile. She gave her rings to Aisha and a forever friendship promise to Saurav in exchange. During the exams I saw her telling them answers with a lot of confidence. It was not that no teacher observed it. Once, it was mathematics exam, she didn't remember the formula and on asking Saurav gave her four-five formulae. She knew that the formula Saurav gave her were not wrong.

But she wrote all of them again and gave it back to Saurav saying "your formulae were wrong."

The invigilator caught her doing all this, he snatched the paper and wrote -5 marks. She argued a lot, but he didn't gave a damn. I was very unhappy seeing the whole drama in front of me.

5# CHALLENGE

The school had declared the results. Next day my father received a call from my school. I went deep thinking what it would be. I thought it maybe Kavita's failure. But it was all the other way round Kavita had to be awarded. She topped with 98% in maths examination. I could not believe, she cheated from Saurav and Aisha but scored more marks than them. How could she do this? It was only possible in dreams to see Kavita as a topper. After that day I was indirectly given taunts on my marks. Everyone in my family said that I was use full for nothing. I knew that the good marks for which Kavita was a good person were not her, they were borrowed from someone else. If she had worked hard and scored the same marks, I would have appreciated her. And now I had no reason for her praise. When our school reopened and I contacted Aisha and Saurav. They were not in a mood to talk, they were very unhappy about their marks. Saurav had scored 81%. I was in a state of shock. Why? What happened? My lips questioned. They told me that, they knew the correct formulae, but when shared with Kavita, she told them that the formulae were incorrect. And most of the questions in the paper had the same formulae to be used. I mean she just used Saurav and Aisha like a tissue. It was such an irritating situation for me to understand that Kavita is not only a bad sister but also a bad person to trust on. After hearing her praise from all around. I took a challenge that I will become a toper in class twelfth with truth being besides me.

6# HUGE SACRIFICE

I was so disturbed by Kavita's presence in my room, so I moved to the guest room. She was very happy as now she had the whole room. I could not tell my parents about her cheating, I wanted to see her in the same tears she gave others. But my mind felt that they would feel upset and there would be a new drama in the house. In twelfth class I forgot all my hobbies as my main hobby was to take revenge from Kavita. I totally had my focus on studies. I was confident about my bright future if I put all my efforts on my education. The whole year or may be ten to eleven months I worked very hard. I was totally into the world of books. In the first term I scored good marks, I fulfilled the promise I did to myself. I topped in Physics and Mathematics. In English, I was at the third position and in chemistry sixth position in the class. I was happy to see a dream where my parents, my family and the school would go praising me. Kavita did not prepare well for the exams. After giving a kick to Saurav and Aisha she had all the classmates away from her. There was no way out for her. I could not believe the result which came out. She scored 61% in mathematics, 50% in chemistry, 68% in English and she had just passed in Physics. Nothing happened according to my thinking. 'I should be praised' was the only thing around my head. I was not given the praise I deserved for my hard work. But they all were in sorrow of Kavita's marks. They didn't stop saying unusual things to me.

"If Kavita had asked you for help, you should have helped her, after all you are her sister." My father said in a state of shock.

Kush said in a very cruel sound "Why will she help her, she is always jealous of Kavita."

I was jealous of Kavita? I was jealous of her, but I realized she had nothing to make me jealous. Instead to praise me on the phone, my relatives were giving my parents confidence, they were singing songs of Kavita's poor marks. I was frustrated. If I did not get very good marks you taunt me and if I got excellent marks you don't even give me a piece of cake. How bad it was. The next thing which made me so angry was IIT.

My parents asked me and Kavita to crack the IIT and use the product of our two year coaching. I cracked it and as usual Kavita didn't. For this also I had to hear.

"Why do you do this, you should help her. Why don't you understand she is your lifelong support, your sister."

My brother shouted at me. I could not understand that a girl who was not my support till past a nineteen years, how will she be my lifelong support. I was asked to take admission in any college and forget IIT. I knew I didn't had the top ranks but at least I had my name in the list. I was not even asked that did I wanted IIT or what. The decisions was taken without hearing my voice. I thought that if I and Kavita were identical twins then I would have also been a pretty girl. This thought had evaporated from my mind that day. I thanked god that I was not Kavita part 2, I had my own unique identity 'Kusum'. Unfortunately which is of no use as nobody listens to me and my heart? I had no other option but to go with my parents. So I had to. I had a good percentage of marks and easily got admission in one of the best university. I was somewhere feeling happy.

One day Kavita crossed all her limits. I was not a small child but she was treating me like that. I was staying in the guest room. I went out for grocery shopping with my mother. When I came back my books, clothes and bed sheets were spread all around. Kavita was standing on my bed.

She shouted at me "Here is your gift from my side, for your success."

This statement showed her feeling of jealousy. I could no more shut my mouth and sit. I had gone through this for past nineteen months and now the water had crossed the maximum level. That day was the first time in my life when I wanted her to thank me.

"Do you even know what all have I given you. Everything you wanted which was mine, I gifted you. I have done so many sacrifices for you. I never complained mom and dad about your stupid tricks. I always helped you. If you take someone's loan then at least learn to thank the person. You are the reason behind everything that went wrong with me. Just because of you I was not given the rewarded for my efforts to achieve such good marks. Just for those people who gave birth to me, brought me up, made me what I am today. It's just for the sake of god, mom and dad."

That one big dialogue of mine brought her into tears. I knew I did something wrong but I had to, she forced me to do. I apologized to her after some days.

7# GOING DEEP WITH TIDES

With time I had started to break into pieces. My heart was working but my mind was not. I had nothing to do the whole day. Except thinking, thinking and thinking. My eyes used to stare every single thing they saw for at least fifteen minutes. In past wherever I was scolded I didn't had tears in my eyes and that day when I heard a single sentence said in anger, my eyes were filled with tears. I could feel myself changing. Physical injuries no more gave me hurt but mental injuries gave me a heart attack. I had no one to be with. I was a very bright student before and slowly-slowly all my brightness was covered by a dark cloud. My studies were at a very high position in my college. I could not find any kind of joy. That smile which was always up on my face had disappeared. The hand which was open for all was always on my lap with folded fingers. The laugh I wore was replaced by silence. Clock was working but for me time was fixed. I was wrapped in the cloth of grief. I had lost my interest and hobbies when I just focused on my studies in class twelfth. The whole day I was in my own world. I was breathing, I could move my hands, I could blink my eyes, I could hear my heartbeat but I was dead. I had four people in my house, still there was no one in my life. I could smell my dead body. I was no longer interested in what kind of food do I eat or what do I wear. During the weekends I would be dressed in the same dress. My step by step fall in academics was visible to my eyes. But I could do nothing to stop it. My parents and even Kavita for that matter were concerned about my behavior. They could sense my condition of depression. I could feel myself sinking into the ocean. I could feel myself going deep with the tides.

8# INTO A NEW WORLD

Kavita and Kush wanted to consult a doctor for me, but my parents had an intention for my recovery. A psychiatrist was consulted. He asked me questions and I could not answer any of them. In the first year of my college I was going under depression. My marks said the same thing. I was day dreaming when my eyes stopped at a girl Anjali. She was very beautiful, in fact more than Kavita. Her facial expressions could not say much, but they stated her living in sorrow. She had her left hand covered with plaster. All of a sudden she received a phone call and started crying. I could just hear her saying "No I am not interested." She kept crying for minutes and then took out her phone, saw someone's photo and smiled. Her smile was as pretty as a flower. After keeping an eye on her, I realized that after a long time I thought so much about someone. I had stopped watching the changes happening in my atmosphere but that day I was really focused on her actions. I was happy to see her working with a smile on her project. After two days I saw her crying again. I could not control myself so I stood up and asked her what was the matter. She didn't replied to me. I felt that I was insulted, but I was not in a condition to shout back at her. I went back to my seat. She must have noticed me after that incident. I saw a hand coming between my eyes and the black-board. It was Anjali. Her first words were "I am sorry. I could not say it. I did not wanted to say that but neither I wanted to share it all. I was depressed about something so I just......"

I asked Why?

She replied with a very humble voice. "As you have no friend, you will not share it with so I can tell you. I had a friend, not just a friend, a best friend. My life is incomplete without him. His name was Druv. A guy with lots and lots of joy. Our group had four children or may be adults. I, Sagar,

Sarita, and Druv were my first priority after my family. Druv was the most important among them. He always advised me the correct thing. He always ordered me to stay away from the evil. My eyes could not see the evil in ones heart or mind but he could. He could sense my mind. My life was his life. We had no secrets. He realized me of my every quality. My parents were happy to know that I had a brother. We met on 6th of august and he was fine. On 9th of august I received a message declaring his death. Between this time we had no contact. It was a murder, at least according to me. You will not believe who was responsible for his death. It was a mosquito. He died of dengue. His platelets were very less. As it was a call from god no one could save him. He died at the age of twenty one."

I could see tears and shadow of death in her eyes. I had lost no one because I didn't had anyone, still I was weeping. My sadness had no reason and her reason was appropriate. That day, I realized what being lonely actually means. After, I could see improvement in myself. Anjali and I became very good friends. I was not as good as Druv but I tried my best to become like him. Anjali was my best friend. Her dazzling smile made her the world's most beautiful girl ever. I had started to live again with her. I felt lucky to have her as my treasure. She was light in my dark life and according to her, I was the same for her.

9# Marriage!!!!!

Marriage is an important aspect of life, especially in the Indian society. If the person is not ready or prepared for marriage, the society forces the person to do so. I was not beautiful and did not had the looks a girl should have. As a result I did not had a marriage proposal too. Seeing my parents in tension just because of me and my marriage I ensured them that I was not in a mood to marry someone. Kavita got proposals from very wealthy families. But she chose the worst person in the world. She had a court marriage as my parents were not willing to give their daughter to a person who is not mentally mature. He was a clerk. And Kavita was madly in love with him. From the very first day of their marriage they had fights. My sister used to have cuts on her body. When my parents gave her the option to register a complaint against him, she was not ready. Kush was also happily married. Everyone was settled and I was not. I felt it a reason to be said, but it was not that every girl in India is happily married. I had no believe in love. Also, I had seen my sister's marriage not working. The only thing I knew about love was presence of understanding between two people. I cannot love anyone but I can understand all. Finally my parents were satisfied. There was a marriage proposal for me. The guy is settled in Singapore. His family was very nice. They believed in rituals and customs. Basically they were from Bhopal, India. My parents were happier than me. Anjali my best friend married a businessman. He had also gone through an incident like her, so they both could understand each other. All of us were now settled in our so called home, our parents were satisfied with their responsibilities.

10# HAPPY ENDING

I had never imagined my life this much good, everything going the right way in my life. Kavita had separated from her husband and lives her life according to her choices. Kush is happy with his own family. My parents are living peacefully with Kavita in Chennai, India. My life was going deep into a ocean. When I tried to find happiness for someone may be an unknown, I also found my happiness. Anjali Was the only one responsible for constructing a new Kusum. I was shaped by her, she is the reason behind my scary laughs. We both are still best friends. She didn't said yes to any of the proposals which came for her, she was waiting for my marriage. When I got engaged, we both got married on the same day. It's been complete two years and we celebrate our marriage anniversaries together. We are friends and great sisters. She made me realize the importance of friendship and existence of a true friend. I no more look back at my past with regrets. All those tears helped me to live better. I pay more attention on my smile than on my weeping eyes. Time passed leaving memories. The laughing memories call me up in the night and make me laugh alone in the bed. The experience life has given me makes me a better person every day. I no longer think about people better than me because I know that everyone is unique. It's really late when we realize what life is, so live every moment.